Gl
Gramophone

Gloria's Gramophone

AKULAH AGBAMI

mammoth

For Loïc, Mattie and Dean with love

First published in Great Britain 1997
by Mammoth, an imprint of Reed International Books Ltd
Michelin House, 81 Fulham Road, London SW3 6RB
and Auckland, Melbourne, Singapore and Toronto

10 9 8 7 6 5 4 3 2 1

ISBN 0 7497 2588 5

A CIP catalogue record for this title
is available from the British Library

Printed in Great Britain
by Cox & Wyman Ltd, Reading, Berkshire

Contents

1 *Rain, rain, go away*

Raindrops were flinging themselves at Gloria's bedroom window – big, fat, splodgy spots that wriggled their way down the windowpane. From her bed, Gloria watched them squiggle and squirm and felt herself sink deeper into gloom with every new arrival. She had counted 872 dribbles but now the window was misting, making her task impossible.

'Some birthday!' muttered Gloria, rolling over on to her back with such gusto that the pillow went bouncing to the floor. It was pink and frilly and part of her mother's ardent campaign to make a soppy-woppy little girl out of her. 'Aaagh!' yelled Gloria, in a modest attempt to lessen some of the frustration and anger that was swelling inside her.

She could have yelled her head off if she'd wanted because the only other person in the flat on her – not to lay too fine a point on it – birthday afternoon was Mrs Fisher, the woman who lived downstairs. And Mrs Fisher had difficulty hearing when you stood ten centimetres away from her, stretched your mouth as wide as it could go, and let rip as loud as your lungs would let you.

'It's not fair, it's not fair, it's not fair!' screamed Gloria, kicking her legs up and down on the mattress so energetically that the whole bedroom quivered and shook. Gloria knew she needn't worry – the people upstairs were spending the week in Blackpool.

It was summer, Thursday 17 August and, instead of body-surfing the waves or winding down with her Walkman on the beach like all her friends from school, Gloria was stuck in Sheffield. Her mother, who worked as an admin assistant for the council, claimed there was no way she could take any holiday until December and then she had some fancy idea of whirling Gloria back to Jamaica for Christmas. Which meant that Gloria would also miss out on the first fun of winter: making slides in the playground and organising snowball fights on the way home . . .

So to cover the difficult summer period when her mum was out at work all day, and someone had to take care of Gloria, Mrs Fisher had been enlisted. Mrs Fisher had two main pleasures in life: coconut bread, which she baked fresh every morning, and television, which she sat in front of every afternoon, munching slice after slice of crumbly, sticky – you guessed it – coconut bread.

Mrs Fisher nodded a lot and even said a few words to Gloria from time to time when the adverts were on but couldn't comprehend that Gloria didn't want to spend the whole of her summer holidays, fifty-three days, staring out of her bedroom window at block upon block of council flats or watching Pucker, her goldfish, sloshing round the giant pink bowl. Gloria wanted to be out and about HAVING ADVENTURES.

The rain didn't help. If there'd been the occasional sunny day, Gloria felt sure she could have persuaded Mrs Fisher to let her run down to the playground for half an hour. But the summer this year was sodden, every day was wet and grey and miserable. No one to play with for weeks and weeks. All her mates were in solitary confinement like herself or on holiday for a couple of weeks in places with, to Gloria, exotic-sounding names like Filey and Brid.

'I want a birthday party!' Gloria had

informed her mum the previous weekend.

'Sorry, love,' her mum had answered. 'You can't expect Mrs Fisher to put herself out and I'll be at work all day Thursday. Anyway, I thought you said all your friends were away.'

Gloria was fuming. As a special concession, her mum had promised to take her to the flicks the following Saturday and let her select the film. Gloria thought she would probably opt for a horror movie – it would be in keeping with the tone of the summer holidays.

'Pucker,' yelled Gloria, jumping off the bed and making a lunge for her confidant and, for these holidays at least, nigh-on best friend, 'I'm so bored, it feels like I'm going barmy!'

Pucker returned Gloria's look and puckered his lips sympathetically. Gloria decided to have another crack at letting him hypnotise her. Yesterday, after gazing into the bowl for an hour or so, she had almost dropped into a trance and was pretty sure that Pucker had been transforming her into a suitable playmate for himself. But today, Gloria had barely settled herself into a meditative position when there came a soft knock on the door.

'The postman jus' drop this,' announced Mrs Fisher, her black hands dusty with coconut flecks. 'Secon' post, secon' comin', you could say,' and she laughed. Gloria walked towards her, puzzling over what was so funny.

Mrs Fisher handed her a large purple envelope addressed in dark green ink with a Jamaican postmark. Gloria ripped it open and pulled out a card with a picture of a group of children and grown-ups dancing on a moonlit beach. Inside, Gloria read the loopy words:

> *Dear Gloria,*
> *Happy birthday!*
> *Don't let the present*
> *Carry you away*
> *Too far, too fast,*
> *Just make it last!*
>
> *A special squeeze,*
> *A special kiss,*
> *From your very own,*
> *Great-aunt Lariss*

There was an unaccustomed stillness in the air and, glancing across to the window, Gloria realised that the deluge had stopped. There was a peculiar yellow haze in the sky which might even mean the sun was trying to come out.

Great-aunt Lariss – of whom Gloria had only the shadowiest of recollections, not having seen her since her last trip to Kingston when she was three – had remembered her birthday. A mysterious present was on its way to Gloria in Sheffield. And just trying to fathom out what it might be would while away a few rainy hours. Things were looking up!

'Fancy a lickle taste of my latest batch of nutty bread?' Mrs Fisher enquired. And even though she had eaten more coconut bread these summer holidays than in the rest of her life put together, Gloria nodded enthusiastically and found herself spontaneously doing something she had not indulged in for a very long time: she was smiling.

2 *Shopping, Susie and skies of grey*

As Gloria trotted behind Mrs Fisher in whirlwind-shopping mode, she was feeling slightly brighter. Naturally the weather had nothing to do with this mood change. This morning the pavements were lightly dusted with drizzle and a light grey mist cloaked the air. But, in actual fact, there were *two* explanations for Gloria's minor lift in spirits.

First, since Mrs Fisher was doing her weekly shop at the market stalls in town, Gloria was looking forward, as she always did, to zipping through Sheffield on the tram. She loved the swishing sound it made and the smoothness of its movements always reminded her of the gliding she sometimes found herself doing in dreams.

Secondly, it was four days since her birthday and the arrival of the tantalising card from Great-aunt Lariss and a million possibilities had whizzed through Gloria's mind as to what the mystery present might be.

To begin with, she'd wondered if it could be a set of brightly coloured woven baskets which would look really good on the shelves beside Pucker. Or even trousers and a top (Gloria prayed that Great-aunt Lariss would have enough sense not to bother sending her a dress!) in hot colours with a headcloth to match. Gloria quite fancied turning up to school in some smart Jamaican ensemble and having all the other girls eying her jealously. Queen of the Playground, even if it would only be a couple of days before another girl rolled in with something snazzier . . .

But neither of those ideas fitted in with what seemed to be a clue in the birthday rhyme Great-aunt Lariss had composed for her:

> *Don't let the present*
> *Carry you away*
> *Too far, too fast,*
> *Just make it last!*

What sort of a present could carry her away fast? A skateboard maybe, or even a bike? Which wouldn't be very exciting because her mum had given her both of those when she was much younger.

'Chile, you jus' goin' stan' lookin' at that t'ing

for the next six hours?' enquired Mrs Fisher, yanking Gloria out of her trance and on to the tram.

Gloria looked about her, feeling rather foolish. Nobody seemed to mind, especially not the woman tram-driver who flashed a friendly smile at her. As Gloria perched herself next to Mrs Fisher who was clutching her shopping bag as though it was crammed full of corals and pearls, she suddenly realised she had found her vocation in life. She too would be a tram-driver, delivering thousands of people every day swiftly and safely to their destination. Swish and glide, swish and glide, swish and . . .

'Gloria, can' you hear me, girl? Get to your feet! We goin' miss the market!' screeched Mrs Fisher, managing in the nick of time to tune in to Gloria's wavelength.

Then Mrs Fisher did her usual. At first, she waltzed leisurely round all the market stalls, jotting down the prices of the items on her list. Then she took a couple of seconds by the tea caravan to sort out a strategy. And finally she moved in for the kill.

The kill consisted of Mrs Fisher whisking from stall to stall, buying orangey-red peppers here, plump mangoes there and giant sunshine plantains somewhere else. Whirling and swirling with the deftness, determination and stamina of a dancer. Gloria scampered along beside her, getting dizzier and dizzier and panting heavily. Had Mrs Fisher, usually so sedentary in company of the telly or taking her time kneading coconut bread, been an Olympic athlete in her younger days? Or been born with superhuman lungs and legs that she only made use of while shopping?

The drizzle grew more insistent and, surprise, surprise, slipped once again into the rain category, and the wind puffed and pulled at the stalls' awnings.

'T'ink we jus' better nip over to the supermarket,' declared Mrs Fisher, shoving a carrier bulging with fruit and veg in Gloria's direction. 'For pick up me margarine an' desiccated coconut,' she added, though this was quite unnecessary.

Gloria grinned. The supermarket was one of her favourite places. They played wonderful music and Gloria generally managed to find herself a fairly quiet aisle and would bop about to the best tracks.

This lunch-time the supermarket was particularly animated since they were in the middle of a French week or *La semaine française*, as they put it. There were little stands where French wine, cheeses and croissants could be sampled. And young women, dressed as majorettes, roller-skated round the place, tempting customers with slithers of French pastries. Gloria had allowed herself to be tempted seven times before Mrs Fisher caught up with her.

'So that's where you got to. Come on, chile, we can' spend all day in this place!' And with that, she dragged Gloria off to soft drinks and plonked a couple of bottles of lime cordial in the trolley.

Not much chance of sneaking off and having a quick bop beside the bird food, Gloria thought disgruntledly. Dances of all kinds, and on occasion even songs, were some of Gloria's greatest pleasures in life ever since she started dancing classes three years ago. But it would take even greater talents than hers to manage to work out any steps to the music that was blaring out of the speakers. Some ancient jazz-sounding stuff in French. What anyone ever saw in that sort of music was quite beyond Gloria.

Which was just what she was thinking as she and Mrs Fisher moved up to the top of the aisle beside the crisps and peanuts and ran smack-bang into Susie and her mum's new boyfriend, Bernie. It seemed like months since Gloria had had a conversation with any of her pals and to come across Susie, her very best friend, in here of all places, was too good to be true!

'Watcha!' exclaimed Susie, who was three centimetres smaller than Gloria, with a mop of curly black hair and giant freckles on her nose and cheeks. 'How's it going?'

'Not the greatest summer holidays I've ever had,' admitted Gloria. 'I'm actually counting the days to the beginning of September. At least there's dance to look forward to.'

'I know,' agreed Susie. 'I can't wait to have another go at tap myself.'

'I wasn't expecting to see you for yonks,' Gloria told her. 'I thought you'd be still lapping up the sun in Rhyll!'

'The baby was bothering my mum.' Susie turned to see if Bernie was anywhere within earshot. He wasn't. 'I reckon this one'll land early. You should have felt it kicking. Anyway, it took my mum all her time to toddle down to the beach and we didn't get to the fairground once. Mum said it made her feel sick just looking at the rides!'

'At least you've been away. I've been stuck in miserable old Sheffield, a prisoner in my own bedroom most of the time . . .'

'Now I'm back, we'll be able to start having fun,' Susie managed to slip in, before obeying the increasingly frantic beckoning of Bernie who was rapidly disappearing down the bottom end of the aisle.

'Come round this afternoon,' Gloria yelled after her and Susie nodded her head, then ran to catch him up.

The idea of fun was something which kept Gloria grinning almost all the way back to the flats. The droplets dribbling down her neck were suddenly neither here nor there. And, if you've got something better to think about, you can ignore carrier-bag handles cutting into your fingers. Even the lift being out of order (again) and all that shopping to drag up three flights of stairs was, for once, just about bearable.

Leaving most of the shopping inside her own door, Mrs Fisher carried one bag of more perishable items into the kitchen. Gloria, who stayed in the doorway, could hear the creak of the fridge. After a few moments, Mrs Fisher resurfaced and the two of them dragged themselves up one final flight of stairs to Gloria's flat.

Gloria was actually feeling quite worn out by the day's activities which probably explains why she was less observant than usual. In fact, being on automatic pilot, her eyes were so firmly glued to the ground that she walked straight into the large crate that had been deposited outside her front door.

Gloria tried to bend down to read the label but was virtually head-butted out of the way by Mrs Fisher, who might well have been an international rugby player in her younger days. Gloria had witnessed before Mrs Fisher's burning passion for other people's packages. She'd put it down to the fact that Mrs Fisher rarely received any letters, let alone parcels.

'Something from the catalogue for Mum, is it?' asked Gloria, articulating so that Mrs Fisher would be able to read her lips.

Mrs Fisher shook her head and smiled at her. 'Gloria Esprit is what it says, if me eyes don' deceive me.' While Gloria's heart started doing the sort of somersaults that only Pucker was capable of in the privacy of his bowl, Mrs Fisher put in, 'All the way from Jamaica, bless me.'

Much too big to be hand-woven baskets, far too bulky to contain a vivid cloth ensemble and completely the wrong shape for either a skateboard or a bike, Great-aunt Lariss's promised gift had finally arrived.

3   *Swallowed in record time*

It was a gramophone, an old-fashioned gramophone made of shiny dark red wood, that Mrs Fisher identified as being mahogany, complete with an enormous golden horn.

Gloria and Mrs Fisher had quite a time pushing and shoving the heavy crate – with the words FRAGILE: HANDLE WITH CARE stamped all over it – as gently as they could into the living-room. Gloria located the hammer her mum always kept beside her bed 'in case of burglars'. It was hard to imagine her mum suddenly leaping out of bed and battering some unsuspecting thief on the head with it, but still, it came in very useful for ripping the top planks off the crate and allowing a very frantic Mrs Fisher and Gloria to put their hands at last on the contents of the crate.

A gigantic mahogany wind-up gramophone with an even bigger shiny horn, a battered leather case containing six dusty (and dull-looking, thought Gloria) black records and another note from Great-aunt Lariss which read:

> *One disc at a time,*
> *No reason, no rhyme,*
> *From Lariss to you,*
> *Don't land in a stew!*

Mrs Fisher was thrilled to bits. 'My, my, my, my!' was all Gloria got out of her for at least fifteen minutes.

She sounds like one of them old records herself – with a crack in, Gloria silently observed, trying very hard to stifle a giggle.

A little later, the Fisher record ran, 'Takes me back to my girlhood. Such a *handsome* gramophone!'

Handsome to Mrs Fisher's eyes, maybe, but what good was an old gramophone to a trend-setting, pulsating young buzzer like Gloria? A Discman was one thing. Gloria would have been able to cruise down the playground, hang around the block and look *in control* with a Discman. She'd have been the first girl in her class to have one. Tongues would have wagged and the whole class would have been ablaze with jealousy. But a gramophone! Did Great-aunt

Lariss think she'd come out of the ark or what?

Gloria tried hard to disguise her disappointment. 'Mrs Fisher,' she bellowed, 'could you help me carry it into my bedroom? I'll, er, surprise Mum with it later.'

Mrs Fisher apparently wanted to go on admiring it and kept reminiscing about her 'girlhood'. But Gloria's mind was made up. She was determined to get the monstrosity out of the way as fast as possible. Mrs Fisher eventually fell for the line that it would be a 'brilliant surprise' for her mum and soon the two of them were shuffling along the hallway to Gloria's room.

Gloria threw her purple dressing-gown over it, much to Mrs Fisher's bewilderment. 'So Mum doesn't see it straight away,' Gloria mouthed by way of explanation.

'Calls for a celebration,' Mrs Fisher remarked as they plodded back along the hallway. 'A fresh batch of nutty bread. What do you say to that, Gloria?'

Not again, groaned Gloria, inwardly. 'Sounds lovely,' she yelled outwardly.

I'll get Mrs Fisher a cake book for her next birthday, decided Gloria, and then realised she hadn't the foggiest idea when Mrs Fisher's birthday was. Though, naturally, Gloria was fully aware that birthdays could be of no significance whatsoever when you got to be Mrs Fisher's age.

Still, she did experience a ripple of guilt when she suddenly realised she knew nothing at all about Mrs Fisher's earlier life. She might have been an Olympic athlete, an international rugby player or a world-renowned *pâtissière* (a word that means cake-maker, as Gloria had discovered from one of the tempting roller-skating majorettes earlier that day).

Gloria had to face up to the fact that, most of the time, she was bored to death with Mrs Fisher, she *loathed* her coconut bread and, to cap it all, she didn't know when her birthday was!

'Mrs Fisher,' Gloria stuck her head round the kitchen door, 'when's your birthday?'

'Chile, what you wan' to know that for? Nex' t'ing, you'll be askin' me my age!' she exclaimed.

But Gloria could see she was secretly as proud as coconut (that inescapable ingredient!) pepper punch and knew she should persevere until Mrs Fisher delivered the date.

'Mrs Fisher, tell me,' Gloria pleaded, at the top of her voice. Just as well the people directly above were on holiday. At least the shouting wouldn't send them off ringing the police for disturbance of the peace!

Finally Mrs Fisher, who had just tipped the contents of the bowl into two large, round cake tins, turned to her. She had a nice face, really. Interesting deep brown eyes and snowy white crinkly hair which she kept plaited and tied in a bun (a coconut bun!) on the top of her head. She had lines on her face which wove themselves down and across and occasionally made Gloria want to play noughts and crosses.

'We could be twins, almos' twins, give or take sixty years,' she confided. Her eyes suddenly seemed bright and alive and twinkling. 'My birthday falls on 22 August!'

For some strange reason, Gloria was utterly stunned. Mrs Fisher's birthday was the very next day!

'So when me see you gettin' in a tangle, gettin' in a mood, it takes me back to me girlhood. The tricks me use' to play!'

Before Gloria had time to react or even to enquire further, the doorbell rang four times. Mrs Fisher's ears didn't pick up the bell so Gloria motioned to the door and rushed down the hall. She struggled slightly with the lock – all in all, she was feeling quite overcome. And then she yanked the door wide open.

Susie, with a card and a small rectangular present, strode straight past her. 'Took you long enough!' she remarked accusingly. 'Decided to nip round with your birthday present. Fancy going down the park?'

Gloria shook her head. 'Mrs Fisher'll never let me. It's raining. I'm beginning to feel like Pucker!'

Susie handed over the present, then made a beeline for the living-room. 'So what pressies did you get, Gloria?' she asked, plonking herself on the yellow settee and almost kicking over the battered leather case that had come with the crate. Before Gloria could utter a word, she demanded, 'Hey, what's this?'

'Oh, nothing. Nothing much,' Gloria lied, aware that her neck and cheeks had suddenly got very hot. A mahogany gramophone is hardly the sort of thing you boast about to your friends.

Susie was not one to be put off. She opened the poppers and eased one of the records out of its brown-paper sleeve. 'I don't believe it,' Susie said. 'Old seventy-eights. You never said your mum collected records.'

'She doesn't', Gloria answered apologetically. There seemed to be no way round it. She was going to have to tell Susie (and risk her spilling the beans to the rest of the class) all about her rotten present. 'I've got this great-aunt in Jamaica. She sent me them for my birthday.' There, it was out in the open now.

Susie opened her eyes incredulously. 'You lucky thing. Still, they're not much use without a record-player. What a pity!'

'I have got a record-player,' Gloria informed her, her tone having adjusted itself, now sounding very matter-of-fact.

Susie looked across to Gloria's mum's worn stereo system. It was in a long wooden box, with built-in speakers, and always made Gloria think of a coffin. 'That's no good,' Susie pointed out knowledgeably. 'It's got to be something that'll take seventy-eights.'

Gloria got to her feet. 'Follow me,' she said simply. 'Can't guarantee that it'll work, but follow me.'

Susie was so intrigued she forgot to insist that Gloria open the card and present and left them where Gloria had placed them, on the carpet. Then she padded down the hallway, record in hand, after Gloria.

Once Susie was poised expectantly, Gloria whipped off the purple dressing-gown, then pulled the gramophone into the middle of the floor.

'It's magnificent,' breathed Susie, and it was. Even Gloria had to admit that, perched on the orange carpet with a rare glint of sunlight making the horn look more golden than ever, the gramophone was quite stunning.

'You wind it up here,' Susie said, grabbing hold of the wooden handle with glee and turning and turning. She certainly seemed to know what she was doing.

Gloria glanced over at Pucker who was swimming frantically round his bowl, a sign that he was hungry. She was quite aware that she hadn't exchanged three words with him all day and he might even start sulking. But she decided to stay where she was on the floor beside Susie and the gramophone right now.

'There!' Susie exclaimed. 'Won't go any further. Now all we have to do is flick this switch.'

The turntable, with a brown velvet cloth, began to spin faster and faster. Gloria just had time to read the words *Her Mistress's Voice* and glimpse a small image of a plump cat curled up on a gramophone.

'Rosetta Ray, ever heard of her?' Susie enquired, handing the record to Gloria.

'"August Sunset", I reckon it'll be jazz.' Gloria tried to sound knowledgeable.

Jazz was something Gloria had always equated with boredom. Old tuneless music with either loud trumpets or loud pianos. How had people survived before synthesisers were invented?

Susie was fiddling about with a small metal box that Gloria hadn't noticed before, selecting a needle, then attaching it to the flat cylinder at the end of the long metal arm which she turned upside down and eased to the edge of the velvet turntable.

'Gramophones are ace!' Susie announced. 'You are up for this, aren't you?'

Gloria had little option but to nod.

Suddenly she had the sensation she usually attached to Pucker putting her in a trance. Although she knew she was still sitting on her orange carpet in the middle of her bedroom, it was almost as though she had begun to dissolve. Helplessly she watched Susie place the record on the spinning turntable. Faster and faster the turntable moved. Then Susie lowered the arm and there was a dull rubbing noise. Gloria could have been wrapped up in cotton wool.

But even cotton wool couldn't protect her from what was to come.

A whirlwind suddenly sprang up in the middle of the room. A whooshing, powerful whirlwind and the eerie sound of a distant saxophone. The wind seemed to gain strength by the second. Gloria felt all her breath was being sucked out of her.

'Susie,' she tried to scream, 'what is it?' But no sound came out.

Susie was waving her hands about. She struggled to get to her feet, no doubt to try to get out of the room.

But a gigantic gust engulfed the room. Gloria had no time to scream. No time to grab hold of the bed legs. Gloria, with her very own eyes, saw Susie get sucked head first into the glinting golden horn. The horror! The horr . . .! Then she felt herself hurtling through the air and into the horn after her.

4 *The meaning of the rhyme*

Long, haunting saxophone notes and a woman's mellow voice crooning 'Au-Au-Au-August sunset . . .' were the only firm things Gloria could hold on to as she was catapulted forward and down.

The whirlwind became a gentle, warmish wind and the thin, spiralling corridor that Gloria traversed varied in colour between mauve and light blue. Except 'corridor' was probably the wrong word. Because the walls, or whatever they were, were flimsy like cloth.

How were they being propelled forward? It felt like Superman in the films, although Gloria didn't even need to stretch her arms out. Somehow – and the word 'magically' sprang to mind – she and Susie were being lifted. But where were they heading for? Susie, several metres ahead of her, kept turning round anxiously and looked as mystified as Gloria herself.

And the strange thing was, even though every couple of seconds Gloria tried to open her mouth to say something, nothing came out. She could hear the music clearly – in fact, by this stage, the lyrics were actually beginning to grow on her, she who'd always turned her nose up at jazz in the past – but that was all.

It was impossible to guess how long the two of them had been flying along. But after a while Gloria found herself bouncing up and down on the air (rather like a car going down a rocky mountainside) and the woman's voice seemed to be running out of steam. The mauve and light blue became red, a thick crimson red, which wafted and swayed.

Before she could stop herself, Gloria did a somersault in the air and landed on a rough wooden floor. A metre away, Susie was doing the same thing, rubbing her bottom on account of the crash-landing.

'Where are we?' whispered Susie. 'What happened?'

'It was that gramophone. Don't you remember? It swallowed us up!' Gloria moved up towards Susie and kept her voice low, too. Wherever they'd landed, at the other side of a giant red curtain they could hear people talking.

'I thought that was it. But then I decided I must have banged my head somehow and dreamt it all. Some dream!'

'It can't be a dream if I'm in it too. Some magic gramophone, more like!'

It was hard to work out where they were. In some kind of large room with one long black wall, a parqueted wooden floor, and a thick crimson curtain that went the whole width of the room. No hole was showing in the ceiling, but when Gloria's eyes adjusted to the light she could make out the markings of a trapdoor – they must have 'dropped in' through there.

Susie looked terrible. Gloria had never seen her so pale, not even when they'd had to do the double spin on the trampolines at circus school last summer. She gave her a sharp nudge. 'Come on,' she instructed quietly. 'We need to find out where we are.'

With that, she jumped to her feet and yanked Susie up with her. She poked her head round the curtain. And when she saw what she saw, she couldn't believe her eyes!

There was a woman, with the biggest brown eyes Gloria had ever come across, wearing a slinky, silky calf-length pink dress with a giant bow, which actually looked quite fetching on her, despite the fact that bows went out of the window *centuries* ago. She was pacing about a little, wringing her hands.

'OK, Mr Reed,' she was saying, in an accent that could have stepped right out of *The Cosby Show*, 'we'll have one more shot.' Then she turned and walked over to a very ancient-looking microphone.

Mr Reed was a tall, thin white man in a smart, pin-striped suit, horn-rimmed glasses, a parting in the middle of his hair (!) and a tapering cigarette holder complete with lighted pale brown cigarette. He took his time answering, blowing a couple of perfectly formed smoke rings into the air before he spoke. His voice reminded Gloria of a whinnying horse, it sounded like he barely used his mouth at all. With the same strong American accent, all the words were expelled through his nose!

'Just be sure to get it right this time, Rosetta. You any idea how much this operation's cost me to date? Time is money, so no more false notes, you understand?'

Rosetta gave a modest shrug of her shoulders, then threw the man a look which seemed to shut him up.

Letting the curtain swish back into place,

Gloria moved back beside Susie. On the other side, she could hear the woman saying, 'Ready, boys? Then let's take it from the top.' Within seconds the strains, the all-too-familiar strains, of 'August Sunset' struck up: drums, piano, saxophone, trumpet, and was that a banjo too?

Susie cast a nervous glance all around, obviously worried in case the whirlwind swooped down and carried them off heaven knows where once again. Though this time there was no need for concern. Not so much as a breeze brushed their cheeks as they settled into enjoying Rosetta's sweet singing.

Though none of it made sense. Why was everybody putting on an American accent? And such peculiar old-fashioned clothes. Not to mention a haircut with a centre parting! Gloria had never come across anything like it. Unless, of course, they were actors and this was all part of some elaborate theatre rehearsal. Perhaps Gloria had read about the production in the *Sheffield Star*. Certainly she'd come across the name Rosetta somewhere recently – such an unusual name – if only she could remember where.

Before Gloria was able to take her musings to the logical, or rather, illogical conclusion, something altogether unpredictable happened. Susie, sitting cross-legged only centimetres away from Gloria, was slowly lifted into the air. It was as though the part of the floor she was sitting on rippled. 'Aaagh!' yelled Susie.

'Cut! Now just who made that racket?' growled a furious Mr Reed from the other side of the scarlet drape.

'Down here, quick as you can!' commanded a voice from beneath Susie. Several pairs of heavy adult footsteps were heading their way. Susie looked queasy. Gloria quaked. 'Down here and snappy!' the voice insisted again.

If Gloria had previously come across the proverb about being caught between the devil and the deep blue sea, she would have appreciated just how apropos it was on this occasion. As it was, casting all caution to the wind, Gloria gave Susie a shove, then leaped after her into the dark hole.

5 The penny drops

The darkness turned out to be five steps. Gloria scraped her foot against one or two of them in her descent and had to bite her finger so as not to make any more racket.

The first thing Gloria could make out at the foot of the stairs were bright eyes shining. She realised they belonged to a young boy with curly hair, more she couldn't see. The boy smiled at her and placed a warning finger to his lips. 'Guess they won't think to check the trapdoor, but you can't be too careful.'

Susie, who was busy rubbing her calf – she'd banged herself on the way down too – nodded in agreement. They could hear footsteps directly above them.

'Nobody here, Mr Reed,' a different man's voice explained apologetically.

'Then back to the drawing board. And this time, there'd better be no more interruptions! That clear?' Reed boomed.

Gloria shivered. What a nasty, miserable, bossy man!

Everyone must have turned round and gone to the other side of the curtain. When the opening bars of 'August Sunset' struck up once more, the boy lit a match and motioned to them to follow. In the flickering light, Gloria could make out the boy's tightly cropped curly hair and his unbelievably wide trouser bottoms. Gloria wouldn't have been seen dead in them!

The passage was thankfully quite short and brought them to a large room. Using his matches once again, the boy fiddled with a light attachment on the wall and then the light – a soft, yellowy light – came on. For a second Gloria was convinced she could smell gas, but then thought she must have imagined it. Not that she'd ever seen anyone switch a light on with a match before, but there was a first time for everything. The room contained bits of equipment, screens and several enormous black leather trunks.

'Take a seat, gals,' the boy invited.

'Listen, pal,' Gloria snarled. 'A little less of the "gals" business, all right? And you don't have to keep putting on an American accent for that matter, either.'

The boy blinked uncomprehendingly. 'Beg your pardon, er, ma'am?' he replied. The American accent was as thick as ever.

Susie was getting impatient too. 'Can't you just tell us who you are, which part of Sheffield we're in, and how to get out of here?' She was looking quite pale and there was a rawness in her tone that told Gloria she was pretty close to tears.

'My name's Willy Ray. I ain't got a clue where this Sheffield neighbourhood is you're talking about. This is Reed's Emporium Studios on 125th Street. And there's an exit right over there.'

'Would you mind repeating that?' Gloria asked, poking out her ears. 'One hundred and what?'

'That's 125th Street, Harlem, New York, the World,' Willy answered, with a grin.

Susie and Gloria plonked themselves on the floor, open-mouthed.

'Come again,' gasped Susie.

'The magic gramophone!' exclaimed Gloria.

'You're not having us on, are you?' insisted Susie.

'Ma'am?' Willy blinked so earnestly that both of them knew straight away that he wasn't.

'We'll have to get a plane back, as soon as poss,' Gloria pointed out. 'My mum and your mum'll go mad if we're not back by tomorrow. Good thing there are plenty of flights between the north of England and New York.'

'Aeroplanes. I've never actually seen one close up,' Willy admitted. 'Can't you get to this Sheffield district by train?'

Susie giggled. 'I've heard of the Channel Tunnel, but a train across the Atlantic is a bit ambitious!'

There was a general air of confusion, during which a terrible thought occurred to Gloria. 'Willy,' she said – her voice had softened a lot, she was frightened of what she might hear – 'what's today's date?'

'Today's 21 August,' he replied steadily.

Gloria's face relaxed a little. 'Yes, 21 August 1995,' she ventured. If they'd somehow been transported to America, that would explain the accent and the peculiar clothes.

'But, ma'am,' answered Willy, getting to his feet. He was beginning to get slightly worked up himself by this point. 'Surely everybody knows this is 1929!' And then he started coughing, a deep hollow cough, and had to sit back down again.

Gloria would have liked to scream the way she occasionally did in front of Pucker when things were getting all too much. She dreaded to think how Susie would take the news.

'I don't believe it,' Susie was saying, her voice barely a whisper. 'Gloria, what have we gone and done?'

6 *The dancing starts ... and stops*

'I'm Gloria,' said Gloria, reaching out her hand. 'And this is Susie. We're from Sheffield, England, and the year for us is 1995.'

'Are you sure?' Willy asked, looking from Susie to Gloria several times. 'You wouldn't be pulling my leg ... ?'

'I wish we were.' Susie shook her head firmly. 'I'm beginning to wish I hadn't brought your present round, Gloria. I mean, we're stuck here now. I'm going to miss my mum's new baby and everything!' She sank despondently on to one of the large leather costume trunks.

'Susie, don't.' Gloria came and sat beside her. 'We'll sort something out, we always have up until now.'

'This is probably the exception.' Susie folded her arms with a sigh.

'Susie, it'll be all right. Great-aunt Lariss sent me a card with the magic gramophone. "Don't let the present carry you away too far, too fast, just make it last." That's what she said.'

'Well, she doesn't mention anything about going home,' Susie pointed out.

'And she doesn't say we'll end up stranded here for ever either. "Just make it last" sounds like we should enjoy what we've got,' Gloria concluded triumphantly.

Willy rubbed his chin solemnly. 'It's kinda hard to swallow, but I can tell you haven't just concocted some crazy story.'

'We didn't make anything up,' Susie retorted. 'One minute we were in Gloria's bedroom listening to a jazz record . . .'

' "August Sunset",' Gloria put in, as if that made things any clearer. 'The next, *zoop*! the gramophone had gobbled us up and here we are.'

Willy was utterly bewildered but obviously thought better than to enquire further. 'My mom's the singer on "August Sunset". She's working on the recording at present.'

So that was what was going on behind the crimson curtain. Gloria reckoned she wouldn't dwell too much on the fact that she had in her possession (back in good old Sheffield) a copy of the record that was currently (right here in

Harlem) being cut. Like all the kids in her class, Gloria had rushed to see *The Terminator*, *Back to the Future* and *Total Recall* and consequently had quite sophisticated ideas when it came to travelling through time.

'And if Mom ever completes the disc to Edward G. Reed's satisfaction – he's our manager, you'll have heard him bawling his head off – we're due to head off on tour on Sunday.'

Gloria was slightly thrown by the last snip of information. Even though she'd only known Willy for the past ten minutes, the thought of him going off and abandoning them . . . well, it didn't bear thinking about.

'What day are we now?' she asked, shakily.

'Wednesday, Gloria. Only four more days to go. Gee, I love touring. A fresh city every few days, a fresh challenge with every show . . .'

'You perform as well, do you?' Susie sounded like she was calming down after her panic.

Fingering his stiff, turned-up collar, Willy filled them in on his life as a child-performer. Sure, touring *was* fun since it involved less work than usual. In New York, Reed forced them to do both a lunch-time and evening performance in a nearby jazz club seven days a week – Willy would join Rosetta for three songs per show. At least they'd have more time of their own in certain places on the northern cities tour.

Gloria's eyes were all aglow. 'You are lucky,' she told him. 'What a life. It sounds so exciting!'

'Gloria, what about you and me?' Gloria could be so hare-brained sometimes, thought Susie. Didn't she realise what a mess they were in? 'Any idea what we're going to do now? Our mums'll be worrying like mad.'

'There's a good chance they won't even have missed us yet,' Gloria answered suavely, using the knowledge she'd picked up from *The Terminator* as a model. 'After all, they haven't been born yet! All of this is a long way in the past.'

Susie sounded relieved. 'Ooh, I hadn't thought of it like that. Does that mean we've got time to fit in Disneyworld?'

'Disneyworld?' Willy echoed. 'That something else I should know about?'

'It's a bit after your time,' Gloria answered, grinning, 'but this is all so weird, Susie, until we know what on earth we're doing here, maybe we should try and make the most of our trip.'

'I'm not being much of a host,' Willy butted in. 'What if you gals . . .' Susie raised her

46

eyebrows and Willy corrected himself '. . . What if you and Gloria came upstairs to the kitchen? All that travelling, you must be real thirsty.'

Now that Willy came to mention it, the girls realised that they were. And not just thirsty, ravenously hungry. In fact, loath as she was to admit it, Gloria could have murdered a slice of nutty bread.

Willy also advised them to change out of their nineties' gear, Susie's skin-tight purple leggings and sleeveless waistcoat were bound to attract attention. There were dresses galore in all shapes and sizes in the trunks.

Dresses! Desperate times call for desperate measures, Gloria told herself, slipping reluctantly into a light blue satin number which actually felt cool and soft against her skin.

Willy, who had been keeping a respectful distance, turned when the girls asked him what he reckoned.

'My, my, my,' he said, slowly. 'A dress sure makes a difference.' And with that, he tossed two pairs of black tap-shoes over to them. 'You kinda need to change shoes too,' he added, eying with distaste Gloria's fluorescent lime-green plastic sandals and Susie's purple and white spotted canvas shoes. 'How are they for size?'

Personally, Susie found her pair a little tight. But if that's all there was, she'd have to put up with minor discomfort.

Willy led them upstairs to an enormous kitchen and uncorked thick green bottles which contained the tangiest ginger beer the girls had ever tasted.

'Hungry?' Willy asked them, offering them a heavy, square tin full of the crumbliest plum cookies.

Several cookies later, Gloria was feeling good, considering. At least this was different. At least it gave her a break from Sheffield and the rain.

'We're dancers too, you know,' she let slip to Willy between munches. 'Mmm, Willy, these are the scrummiest biscuits. Thanks a mill.'

'And acrobats!' added Susie, who had also been cheered up by the cookies.

'Really?' said Willy, a touch over-politely.

So he didn't think they'd be up to much? Considered his own performance skills were bound to be superior, eh? 'Come on, Sooz, let's give Willy a demonstration.' Gloria sent Susie a fat wink.

'"Jungle Jamboree", is it?' Susie asked. 'After three: one, two, three!'

Having a pair of tap-shoes on made things a lot easier, helped bring their shared moment of artistic fulfilment easily back to mind. June in the City Hall, no less! Thousands of people had turned up and applauded and applauded . . . That had made three years of dragging themselves out of bed on a Saturday morning more than worth it!

If Gloria closed her eyes, she could see the misty, high dance-school window with a crack along the pane, hear the snappy tapping of fifteen pairs of tap-shoes that had rehearsed for weeks and weeks.

Every single twist and turn, every last slide and shuffle of the contemporary dance routine oozed easily from her body, from both their bodies. It was pure delight. Every movement razor-slick to the irresistible Ghanaian tune they could still hear so clearly inside their heads.

It was like being woken up when, at the end of the piece, Willy clapped his hands together noisily. 'Gee!' he exclaimed. 'You two sure can dance. Never seen anything quite like that before.'

Hardly surprising, Gloria observed to herself. In effect, Willy had just been treated to a preview in the fullest sense of the term. Sixty-six years ahead of itself.

By now, Susie was raring to go. 'We could have a bash at "Storm", if you like. I know there's only the two of us . . .'

Gloria needed no prodding. 'Yeah, let's go!' she said.

So there they were, bopping and gyrating in the middle of the kitchen, too wrapped up in the arduous steps of 'Storm' to pay any heed to the creaking kitchen door. Which is why, seconds later, they were completely flustered to find themselves face to face with Edward G. Reed.

'Sir,' began Willy, his voice oozing respect, 'may I introduce Gloria and Susie? They've just arrived from, er, the north.'

Mr Reed was considerably more concerned with pouring himself a beer.

'And, what's more, sir, as you can see, they're dancers. Perhaps you'd have time to watch them run properly through a couple of numbers this evening?' Willy ended, hopefully.

Mr Reed banged the empty beer bottle on to the table. 'Rather skinny to be dancers,' he commented dismissively, then strode noisily out of the room.

Gloria and Susie reckoned their chances were extremely thin but Willy reassured them, pointing out that it was quite normal for Reed to be so grumpy. Even if he'd just signed the greatest act this side of the equator, he'd find something to moan and groan about. Then, since there seemed to be no further point in hanging around the studio, they walked out into the warmth of early evening, into the mystery of the past.

And the hustle and bustle! Gloria had had no idea what to expect, but certainly not so much movement and noise. 'Thought things were meant to be slower for your generation,' she yelled as they hovered, waiting for a gap in the endless stream of vintage cars. If Harlem streets at five o'clock were anything to go by, she was way off mark.

The streetcars and trolleybuses reminded Gloria of a trip she'd gone on with her mum to the Transport Museum in Bradford. So these contraptions could actually move! And chock-a-block full of passengers.

'Here, Gloria, I thought rush hours were a modern invention,' Susie was saying.

'So did I,' Gloria admitted, weaving in and out of a troupe of office workers. This was like being slap-bang in the middle of one of the black and white films shown at weird times on weekend television, the Buster Keaton and the Keystone Kops ones. The scene she beheld (a nice archaic expression like that seemed totally appropriate) could have come straight out of an old movie. Except, of course, nearly all the people toing and froing were black. Black people in stunning frocks and suits, and hats, hats, hats, everywhere.

Willy led them to his house, or rather, his flat, or rather, his apartment, as he put it. It was situated in an old, tall house on a wide street lined with chestnut trees, whose green-orange leaves were like giant parasols, providing sudden clumps of shade.

Outside his front door, four girls about Susie and Gloria's age were playing skipping games and doing fancy movements with their feet.

'January, February, April, March. Tell me the name of your sweetheart,' they chanted. 'W-i-l-l-y, W-i-l-l-y,' they sang out, then collapsed on to the pavement, laughing.

'Gimme a break, gals,' Willy answered good-humouredly. Gloria, on the other hand, had the distinct impression it had been more directed at them than at Willy.

As they walked down the long hallway, their footsteps echoing on the blue rectangular tiles, they could hear the girls reciting, 'Sausage in a pan, sausage in a pan, turn around, turn around . . .'

Up two flights of stairs. Unlocking the door, Willy said to them, 'Don't go expecting anything fancy. Mum and I don't earn enough. It's real simple – basic, you might say.'

But it wasn't. There were beautiful floral drapes at the window that rocked and swayed in the slight breeze. There was a shiny, octagonal, black table with four blue wicker chairs, a square of deep green carpet printed with golden roses and in the corner, beside a smaller table with a wrought-iron lamp on it, there was a polished rocking-chair.

'Can I?' asked Susie, and she leaped into the rocking-chair, snuggled down on the plump patchwork cushion and rocked herself backwards and forwards.

'It's from the south. Mom was born in Tuscaloosa, Alabama. When she left, it was the only possession she brought with her. That and her voice.' Willy spoke with sadness. Gloria, being of a curious disposition, wondered if, one day, she'd get to know more about his life.

They were in the middle of a cosy chat – well, actually, it was more like a language class. Willy thought Gloria and Susie should draw as little attention to themselves as possible, which meant watching how they spoke. Willy advised them to stick to monosyllables, to say just one word whenever they could, and, if possible, to coat everything with an American accent.

'Sure,' Susie drawled, her eyes all laughter.

'You bet!' Gloria spoke through her nose, then put her hand to her mouth. 'Oh, no, two words. Sorry, you guys!'

Gloria was thinking that they'd been lucky to meet up with Willy. He certainly seemed keen for them to enjoy their stay in Harlem.

'If you'd like to freshen up, while I prepare another drink, we'll probably have time to take in one or two of the sights before your audition at the Wild Cats Cabaret.' Willy had everything under control.

'Pardon?' Gloria almost shouted at him. 'Who said anything about an audition?'

'I was trying to figure out the best arrangement . . .' Willy began.

'Well, you could have asked us how we felt about it all. Honestly!'

'You mean, you think we might be able to go on tour with you?' Susie always saw a different side of things from Gloria. Susie could just see it now, the floodlights, the crowds, the nightly bouquets, their own star dressing-room . . . 'Gloria, if they want us, we should give it a whirl,' she said. 'The chance of a lifetime.'

Gloria huffed and puffed and was not so sure.

The idea hadn't come from her. Still, a glass of the fizziest lime and lemonade put a slightly different complexion on things. Half an hour later, Gloria had been persuaded to join the others for a stroll through the Harlem streets.

They moved into a part of Harlem with narrower streets and Willy led them towards a building that looked like an abandoned factory. He stood back to let them enter. 'Welcome to Loulou's Cave,' he said.

It was a sort of covered market, full of hundreds of tiny stalls, selling everything from monkeys to necklaces, leather bags to fresh fish. There were cafés where weary people were drinking from steaming cups while listening to one of the many musicians and singers. Gloria had never seen such strange instruments – had people made them themselves? And such a variety of music. From heavy, lolling ballads to light, flickering dance tunes that made you want to tap your feet.

'Calypso,' Willy told them as they walked past the teenage quartet that had attracted quite a crowd. 'You like it?'

'I've never heard anything like it,' Gloria admitted. 'It's ace!'

So many things to listen to, to see. It was like

an old-fashioned Meadowhall Shopping Centre — but a million times more exciting.

'How long does it stay open?' Susie wanted to know. It was after seven and the stall-holders had lit little gas lamps so they weren't about to start packing up. And the place was swarming with customers.

'Another couple of hours. Gives people who work a chance to get their shopping done.' Willy coughed slightly, leading them out of a back door and into a quieter street. 'Nearly there now.' He pointed to a shining blue sign. 'That, for your information, is the Wild Cats Cabaret.'

8 *The outcome of the rave*

The Wild Cats was an impressive little joint. In fact, it turned out to be one of the top Harlem clubs. There were giant palms, lacy tablecloths and delicate glass table lamps, chunky velvet chairs and carpets fifteen centimetres thick. Before they could even sit down a waiter in top hat, tails and white gloves appeared with three large fruit cocktails. Like a dream come true!

'Pinch me, Susie, pinch me,' Gloria whispered, forgetting all about her reluctance to dance.

They didn't have long to wait. Reed called them over after five minutes. The band, all sixteen of them, including a banjoist called Teagarden who winked encouragingly when they clambered on stage, started playing a pacy dance number. They began with the steps of 'Jungle Jamboree' which didn't quite fit the rhythm. So, like the jazz musicians, they improvised. Mr Reed and all the musicians actually applauded them at the end of the performance. And they hadn't needed to run through anything else.

'You girls call by my office in ten minutes,' Reed said, puffing on a plump cigar. And, there and then, they sealed the deal and downed another fruit cocktail which was 'on the house'.

To be signed as dancing-girls to tour America, that was beyond even Gloria's wildest imaginings. When they landed back at Willy's place after the audition, they were buzzing like bees.

'It was brill, ace, fab!' Susie was exclaiming at the top of her voice. 'What a team!'

'You were just great. I knew Reed wouldn't let such an – ' Willy paused a second ' – an unusual act slip through his fingers.'

'I woke up this morning bored out of my mind. And tonight I've signed a contract to tour America sixty-six years ago. It's all a bit much,' Gloria admitted. 'I mean, how long are we going to be here and any ideas how we get back home?'

'I don't reckon we'll be able to catch a plane.' Susie was a little put out that Gloria's mind was on serious things. 'It'll have to be the same as we came. We'll have to find another magic gramophone.'

'They'll be ten a penny, I'm sure.' Gloria's tone was cutting.

'Come on, you two. Relax and look on the bright side.' Willy leaned back on the blue wicker chair, his arms behind his head. 'You'll get board, lodging, a small amount of wages and to travel with the show . . . and more time with me! You could hardly ask for more!'

Gloria tossed the plumped-up patchwork cushion straight at Willy's nose. He even took that in his stride and just laughed. 'I'm working late tomorrow night, so I guess I'd better hit the sack. Let me get you some bedding and show you your room,' he offered.

They lay in the feather-soft bed, whispering about their day. Gloria was feeling much brighter. She began to see that the dance job was a means to an end. They'd be having a good time while saving up some money to buy themselves a – fingers crossed – magic gramophone. And if they couldn't buy one they might spot one somewhere on their travels.

Susie was tripping place names across her tongue. Philadelphia, Baltimore, Washington, Richmond, Cincinnati, Columbus, Picturing, Cleveland, Detroit, Chicago. A whistle-stop ten-town tour that would take two months to complete.

'Wonder what their trains are like? And as for the tent shows, can you imagine?' Susie's excitement rose again.

To be perfectly honest, Gloria could not. For the life of her, she couldn't fathom out what a tent show was, unless it bore some vague resemblance to a circus show in a big top. But she was not one generally to show her ignorance.

She just lay there quietly wondering what it all meant. If they'd landed in – or rather been brought to – Harlem in 1929, it might be for a reason. A mystery to be solved, a problem to be sorted out, some assistance to be given. Whatever the score, they'd landed themselves a job. It was all looking very promising. Gloria tumbled into a contented sleep, convinced they were on the brink of THE BIGGEST ADVENTURE OF THEIR LIVES.

9   *The New York to Philly express*

Four very hectic days later (costumes, some sightseeing and general acclimatisation), Willy was bundling them out of the apartment door and into the street that was bathed in soft, golden, morning light. Gloria was still suffering from gramophone-lag and never had a clear idea what time of day or night it was meant to be. But compared to the rush and bustle of previous days, Harlem was just stretching its arms, yawning and welcoming the day. Even in her own semi-sleepy state, Gloria was aware it must be *very* early in the morning.

'Willy, any idea what time it is?' she asked him. Both Susie and herself were having to jog to keep up with him.

'It's 6.30. The train leaves in forty minutes. You'll have to move faster than that, gals!'

'No wonder I'm shattered,' Susie yelled across at her, between pants.

Once they were safely installed on the bright

green streetcar with wooden benches, Willy took the time to explain. The rest of the troupe would be travelling on the 9.30 New York to Philadelphia train. Train trips were when they all tended to catch up with each other, where gossip was exchanged and new recruits welcomed.

'Can't have you giving too much away about your backgrounds, where you're from,' Willy went on.

'Every time we open our mouths feels like it's a giveaway . . .' Susie said.

'Exactly,' Willy replied, putting all the emphasis on the 'ex' part. 'Which is why you two need to keep your heads down until you're a little more clued up.'

'I can't believe we're off on tour,' Gloria giggled, bouncing up and down on her seat, which was making a creaking noise.

'Yippee!' Susie was in high spirits, too.

Within minutes they were alighting at Grand Central Station. Gloria had a soft spot for large stations generally. There was something grandiose and spacious about the buildings, not to mention the general tingle of excitement that came from so many people dashing to get themselves elsewhere . . .

But Grand Central was, as they say, out of sight. Partly because it was simply too gigantic to be seen in one go and partly because it was so beautiful. The imposing white stone, the steps leading up to it, reminded Gloria more of a cathedral than a station. Inside there were thick, tall columns and a shiny marble floor and so much space!

'Pity we didn't bring our skateboards with us,' Susie exclaimed, pointing to the same inviting space which was just crying out for a skip, a twirl and a twizzle or two.

'Mountain bikes would be great with all those steps too,' Gloria answered, wondering where Willy had scurried off to.

He was over in the ticket queue and, as the girls hovered close by, they noticed several shoeshine boys and girls touting for customers. They wore navy blue uniforms, cream shirts and shiny button-up shoes. And none of them looked older than eleven. What Willy had said about kids working younger here was true.

'Fifteen minutes to departure,' Willy called across. 'You two up for muffins?'

Generally speaking, they were always up for food and they trotted after him towards the coffee shop which was all polished oak tables and sturdy wooden chairs.

'Coo-ool!' Gloria said emphatically, gesturing to the station hall and trying to express herself, as Willy had suggested, in single words.

'It's kinda early in the day. It'll get hotter later on. Bound to.' Willy settled into his seat.

Gloria grinned. 'Is that after your time? Cool? It's an Americanism, I know that, meaning "amazing, wonderful, brill". People can't have started using it yet.'

'Cool?' Willy repeated. 'It does kinda roll off the tongue. I gotta remember that. Thanks, Gloria, or may I call you Glo?'

'Glo! That's a good one.' Susie thought it was hilarious.

'And I believe you're sometimes known as Sooz,' Willy retorted, putting her in her place.

But Gloria quite liked it actually. Glo. Nobody had ever thought of shortening Gloria's name before. It made her think of the moon in the night or of a fire crackling bright. Glo. It seemed to fit her somehow.

They gobbled down food, then trundled down the steps to platform fourteen. The train, a giant, shiny, black, steam locomotive, was already puffing and heaving on the platform.

Willy had bought them all second-class tickets.

'All aboard now, all aboard,' a wiry black train guard invited.

'We only just made it. You two've sure taken to American cakes,' Willy gasped. 'It's a good thing they were out of blueberry muffins, otherwise I guess we'd have missed the train!'

'It's called research, Willy. Sociological research,' Susie joked.

'A taste of the past.' Gloria stroked the rich purple fabric of her comfy seat. 'Cor, this beats British Rail,' she added appreciatively. There were fringed lamps on every wooden table and the carpet perfectly matched the chairs.

From somewhere on the platform a shrill whistle blew. Almost immediately the train began to lurch slowly along the platform.

'Philadelphia, here we come!' Willy whooped, placing his brown peaked hat firmly on the table in front of them.

10 *Home-made cherry ice-cream,*
no less

'One, two, three, one, two, three, swing those sticks over your head,' the dance-mistress barked. 'Heel, toe, heel, toe, heel, toe, spin, spin and splits!'

It was five o'clock and Gloria and Susie were among the eight girls rehearsing in the Little Holland Theatre, Philadelphia. The tour was due to open the following night and they were expected to assimilate five new dance-routines, including two song and dance numbers. Gloria, who deep down had fantasies of becoming a female Michael Jackson, was in her element even though the songs were pretty soppy.

'You,' Mrs Hailsham continued, pointing an accusing finger at her, 'we'll have you in the front-row line-up for the next one. Positions, everyone, for "Wedding of the Painted Doll".'

'Lucky you,' Susie hissed under her breath.

'Put some life into it,' beamed the indefatigable Mrs H. 'You're happy little bridesmaids and your hour has come!'

Pull the other leg, thought Gloria, giving Susie a quick wink. This one's got bells on it. Actually, it hadn't. It had long, frilly camiknickers, the costume for the first number which was the French cancan. Gloria had seen it done by the dancers at the London Palladium on the television a couple of times but she never thought anyone would rope her into doing such a stupid dance. At least, with contemporary (1990s contemporary, that is) dance, you could express meaningful things.

After the rehearsal, during the walk back to the boarding-house with Willy, Gloria's legs were so worn out that they were squidgy and trembling and her back felt as if it was disintegrating with every step.

'I was in one of the back halls working out with Mom most of the time. But, from what I saw, you two did fine,' Willy told them encouragingly.

'Sure,' Susie said with a deliberate slur. 'Only trouble is, the way I'm feeling now, I'll never be able to dance again!'

'Come on, Sooz,' Willy encouraged. 'You'll both be great.'

And after a wash and a rest at the Golden

Way Guest House, they both felt lively enough to hit the town. Mind you, the promise of ice cream might have had something to do with that.

'And, what's more,' Gloria remarked, as they strolled across the wide bridge over the Delaware River towards the city centre, 'you never mentioned us being danced half to death.'

'Yes. My leg muscles feel like lead as well,' Susie chipped in.

'Heard the one about the two gals from Sheffield who travelled through time and thought they were real cold?' Willy teased.

'You mean "cool", don't you?' Gloria corrected and they all collapsed into laughter.

They continued to lark about in the tea shop, as they drank hand-mixed banana milk-shake and guzzled home-made cherry ice-cream.

'You claim life's so totally different but what have you got in the nineties that we haven't?' Willy grinned.

'Colour TV and video, for starters,' Gloria told him and proceeded to launch into such a technical explanation that he thought she was pulling his leg.

'Then there's rockets and satellites. People have landed on the moon, you know,' Susie went on.

'Pardon?' Willy said, making fun of their accents. 'Surely you don't expect me to fall for that one?'

'It's computers that are responsible. They can keep things in their memory that would wear us out.' Gloria tried to explain it all as simply as possible. But Willy couldn't even begin to imagine what a computer was, let alone grasp that Gloria and Susie, thanks to Craft, Design and Technology at school, both knew how to operate one.

'Our lives are worlds apart, Willy, can't you see?' Susie said. But how could he? He had only strange new words to hold on to. How could Willy compare his present and the distant future?

Gloria could see that the situation was far from cut and dried. Some things were better in the nineties, some things were better now. And it's all very well philosophising, but sometimes the only thing to do is take advantage of what's to hand. Home-made cherry ice-cream, for example, of which they all had triple helpings!

11 *Homesick blues and sweet dreams*

They hung out in the tea shop until closing-time at eight o'clock. Then Willy took them back to the boarding-house by a different route, through winding, cobbled streets. Houses huddled close together with flower-boxes crammed with reds and blues on the windowsills. The city's mood was mellower than the hurry of New York.

After all that dancing and with another heavy day in store tomorrow, they decided to get ready for bed. The girls had a quick all-over wash (you were lucky to get a bath once a month, according to Willy) but couldn't brush their teeth. Toothbrushes hadn't yet been commercialised, Gloria's mum would be horrified to learn. It was hard to imagine what her mum would be up to. Wherever she was. Whatever time it was back in Sheffield. Gloria swallowed hard to get rid of the lump in her throat and rubbed her smarting eyes. Maybe that's what made Gloria spot that one essential background ingredient was lacking.

'There's been no rain, that's what it is!' Gloria exclaimed loudly. So loudly in fact that another of the dancing-girls, who was sleeping in the room next door, banged on the wall.

After daily downpours in Sheffield for months, here it hadn't so much as drizzled since they'd 'flown' in. Not one single raindrop! Was she homesick for Sheffield weather?

'You all right, Susie?' Gloria whispered when they were both tucked up in bed.

'Just hope my mum's not worried sick,' Susie told her.

'We've been through all that,' Gloria reminded her. Then they both fell fast asleep.

Gloria dreamed Pucker and Mrs Fisher were singing 'August Sunset' together on-stage at the City Hall. And Mrs Fisher was saying free coconut bread would be served during the interval after which Gloria Esprit would perform a rendition of 'Wedding of the Painted Doll'. Oh no, thought Gloria, I want to do 'August Sunset'! Which woke her up.

And it was morning. Susie was nowhere to be seen. Gloria quickly dressed and went down to the parlour where a disdainful Mrs Gold informed her breakfasts were served up to nine o'clock in her establishment.

Gloria shrugged and purred 'Sure', and was about to go look for Susie in the bathroom when Mrs Gold brandished a letter at her. 'The young man left you this.'

A note from Willy telling her he'd had to go into the theatre for an early rehearsal with some of the band. He'd see them later.

No sign of Susie in the bathroom or anywhere else in the house for that matter. Gloria grabbed her tap-shoes from under her bed and dashed out into the sunny morning street. For the first time since this weird adventure had begun, Gloria found herself (till this afternoon's rehearsal, at any rate) left to her own devices. Gloria recognised an opportunity when she saw one. The time had come to explore!

12 *The first night . . . and* more *ice-cream*

It was the museum that acted like a magnet and drew her mysteriously towards it. Before Gloria knew it, the broad, two-storey building had swallowed her up.

Once inside, she was glad she'd come. There was an exhibition of black painters from New York. 'Harlem Renaissance Heights', it was called.

It was magnificent! Room after room of paintings depicting colourful scenes (colourful being the word – Gloria had never seen such an array of colours: different shades of maroon and lilac and emerald green and fuchsia and azure blue and brown and black and yellow – dozens of different shades of yellow!) from the lives of black people.

A lot of the paintings were country scenes with elderly people. These felt sad, as if they were saying the cotton and the cattle and working the land had been left behind by most people forced to find work in the city.

But the city scenes were so alive. The people almost looked as if they were wriggling on the canvas. Street scenes and club scenes and station scenes and the inside of apartment scenes. One artist, Clara Simmonds, had a way of painting that made the eyes seem to watch Gloria wherever she moved and the hands look as if they could reach out of the canvas and tickle her. Gloria felt as though she were seeing hands and eyes for the first time in her life.

'Do you like them?' enquired a deep voice beside her.

Gloria nearly jumped out of her skin! She'd been so absorbed in the paintings, she hadn't heard anyone enter the room. And she was in for another surprise when she turned to see who had spoken. For the voice was none other than Teagarden's, the banjoist with the band.

'Amazing!' Gloria eventually answered in her best American accent, sticking to single words as Willy had advised.

'So this is what our dancing-girls get up to in their free time!' Teagarden joked. 'At least you have taste, my dear.'

Of all the millions of Americans she could have encountered in the museum, it was just her luck to bump into someone she vaguely knew who seemed intent on asking her lots of questions. How long would she be able to keep up her phoney American accent anyway?

'This is one of my favourites,' Teagarden admitted, pointing out a large painting of a black couple drinking tea in a tea shop that was swarming with plants. They seemed to be in the throes of an argument.

'Mmm,' said Gloria, hoping that sounded convincing.

'I'll bet you can guess why,' Teagarden grinned, covering the painting's title with his broad hand.

Gloria shook her head.

'"Teagarden", that's its name. Same as me! And we's both from Harlem!' He laughed, a gentle, mellow laugh. He seemed like a nice man if a bit persistent. Every time she tried to pace about the room independently, Teagarden would stalk after her. 'So you from New York, Miss er . . .?'

There would be no shutting him up, Gloria could see that. 'Gloria, Gloria Esprit,' she said flatly.

'That's a pretty name . . .'

Gloria pretended to notice the clock. 'Rehearsal!' she yelled before any more conversation could be extracted from her. She charged out of the room and all the way to the theatre just in case Teagarden decided to accompany her.

Susie was there when she dashed in.

'What happened to you?' Gloria wanted to know.

'Just nipped out for an early morning walk. When I got back there was no sign of you.'

Gloria laughed and told her about her adventures at the museum. They were going to have to keep themselves to themselves, just smile and look blank, otherwise their secret would come out.

The rehearsal went well, then they had a break for something to eat. And soon it was time to get their make-up on and all the right gear for the performance. They hadn't seen Willy all day. He'd been rehearsing with Rosetta elsewhere. About half an hour before the show was due to start, Willy stuck his head round the dressing-room door.

'Now will you get a load of that!' he exclaimed at the sight of them. 'Stun-ning!'

It was true. They did look completely different (a far cry from their nineties' leggings!) in their bottle-green crêpe-de-chine dresses, with a swishy skirt and lots of petticoats underneath, and their hair swept to the side.

'Thanks,' said Gloria, who was rarely at a loss for words. But the transformation was pretty overwhelming.

Suddenly Willy broke out coughing and had to sit down. Susie tapped him a few times on the back and Gloria zipped off to get a glass of water.

'You all right?' Susie asked.

Willy, still spluttering, sipped some water. 'Oh, that's better. It's my chest.' He gave it a good hearty knock. 'Break a leg, both of you. You'll have them standing on their seats.' And with that he breezed off to get dressed himself, leaving Susie and Gloria's knees to knock and teeth to chatter.

The pair of them managed to work themselves up into a state of nervousness that proved quite unnecessary because the performance went better than chocolate fudge cake and cream. The performance went like a dream!

At eight o'clock prompt, the lights in the old Victorian theatre went down and the audience sighed expectantly. When they came up, Rosetta was centre-stage in a sequinned white gown, blue light on the floor, mauve light on her. Gloria had never seen anything so beautiful. Rosetta swayed and sang her way through the first song, a haunting, slow melody, 'Satin Night'. The audience applauded enthusiastically.

Then the mood changed with an up-tempo tune, 'Those Swingin' Things'. The band was wonderful but Gloria couldn't help thinking Rosetta's voice was better suited to the slower, more melancholy numbers.

Exit Rosetta, enter the Sunbeams, which was the yucky name that someone had come up with for Gloria, Susie and the other dancing-girls.

Even if the name was revolting, the Sunbeams section itself was fab! To start off with they did a song and dance number, more dance than song, 'The Alabama Blues'. The audience loved them. They moved on to a sad song with no dancing, 'Oh, Daddy', about a man who'd been killed in the war. Gloria found it a bit depressing to sing but, judging from the audience's reaction, it was right up everyone's street. They concluded the section with a dance number with chanting: 'Strawberry, raspberry, apricot, lime', which had the audience rocking from side to side, clapping their hands and joining in the chorus.

Gloria and Susie danced their hearts out. They might be the new ones but they were determined not to give any of the other girls any excuse for saying they'd let them down, or spoilt things, or had two left feet or worse. So far, so good!

The band took over for a time, and Gloria realised she was actually starting to develop a taste for jazz.

Then it was Willy's turn. Gloria and Susie had never succeeded in persuading Willy to let them see a bit of his act so they watched excitedly from the wings. He was dressed in a dark blue suit and looking quite the star. Not surprisingly, he did a comic number, 'Fingers and Thumbs', which involved lots of acrobatics. Gloria had no idea that Willy was so versatile. Off-stage, underneath all the joking about, he often came across as being shy. Here, he was in his element. The audience laughed and cheered him and Gloria felt proud to bits.

The second half opened with the Sunbeams and 'Wedding of the Painted Doll'. Gloria and Susie were really getting into their stride. Dance, sing, the warmth of the lights on your skin, applause. This was the life.

Then Rosetta, in a tight, backless, red dress,

tottered back on-stage. 'I'd like to introduce my son, Willy Ray,' she announced proudly. More applause. Two sad duets followed, 'Rainbow Promised Land' and 'How Do I Know (You Love Me)?', which had the crowd roaring and made Gloria sniff a little. Even if Willy and his mum saw virtually nothing of each other during the day (which reminded Gloria of her and her mum), at least on-stage they had perfect rapport.

A couple more solo tunes from the band and then the finale with Rosetta, in her full splendour, launching into the unforgettable 'August Sunset'. A rain of applause greeted the opening bars. It was faultless and haunting and made Gloria's spine start to tingle. No wonder the crowd went wild at the end. No wonder Reed came striding round, puffing cigar smoke at all and sundry, saying, 'Great show, great show, everyone. Good work.' The City Hall was nothing compared to this sense of euphoria.

So of course they decided to go out and celebrate with ice-cream. Lime and pistachio this time, which Willy claimed eased the tickle in his chest.

13 *A sad Cincinnati night*

Three and a half weeks into the tour a certain routine had developed. They would all spend a portion of the morning or afternoon, when they weren't rehearsing, winding down or doing a spot of exploring together. The past few cities Willy had left them to it and gone back to the guest house for a rest. He seemed to be tired all the time and had lost a lot of his bounce. Maybe the tour was taking its toll.

Cincinnati was the next stop and they were due to spend four nights there. Sitting on the train well away from the rest of the troupe, Gloria was chatting to Susie about home. 'Mum's always going on about how young people grow up much faster now than when she was young. But, look – ' She pointed to a girl, who couldn't have been older than eleven, caring for three very small children.

'Know what you mean,' Susie answered. 'They've got loads more responsibility than us.

Everyone's working at our age. I mean, take Willy . . .'

'What's this I hear?' Willy asked, making his way down the carriage.

'Just talking differences,' Gloria told him in a low voice.

'And feeling homesick,' Susie threw in for good measure. 'You any bright ideas, Willy, as to how we get home?'

'Ask me again in six weeks' time when the tour's over. I might have come up with something by then.' His voice was strangely croaky.

For a while they sat just staring out of the window, not saying anything. Gloria was thinking some more about her home. Missing her mum kissing her good night. It would have been such a different trip if her mum had been sucked up into the gramophone too. Gloria grinned at the thought of her mum as a dancing-girl!

'We've seen so many places, been to so many sights, done so many things.' Susie interrupted her thoughts.

Which wasn't strictly true. The 'sights' they were attracted to, now that Gloria was steering clear of museums, tended to be tea shops, ice-cream parlours and the occasional park. But they had managed to drag themselves along to the Capitol in Washington.

'This'll be your first tent show,' Willy reminded them. Reed's Rollicking Rhythm Show under canvas. It would be bound to create a different atmosphere. 'Oh, by the way, this is the name of your hotel.' He handed Susie the card. 'They're putting us guys up a few streets away. I'll call round when you're settled in.'

'You're wrecked, Willy. We'll come round to you in the morning.'

Their accommodation turned out to be a small family hotel along Cade Long Alley, ten minutes' walk from the station.

'It's a fine neighbourhood,' the woman at the station assured them when they asked for directions. 'The kinda place where two girls would feel happy staying. You two with the show then?'

Gloria liked the sense she occasionally got of being a celebrity. Maybe that's what she'd do full-time when she grew up; if she ever got home. Gloria Esprit, singer and dancer *extraordinaire*.

'Gloria, this way!' Susie was tugging her

sleeve impatiently. And once Gloria had awoken from her daydream, they found Cade Long Alley without any bother.

It was a street full of ramshackle old houses with tiny wooden balconies and sprawling gardens up the front. One house had been painted peppermint green and pink and Gloria automatically headed towards it, only to find a hand-painted notice on the gate which read: *Dr E. B. Mitchell, General Practitioner*. Lewises' Family Hotel was next door.

The bedroom Mrs Lewis ushered them to was neat and cool. Mrs Lewis was busy explaining that, for an extra eighty cents, they could be sure of a nourishing evening meal. Gloria was in the middle of consulting with Susie on this most important issue (food!) when her attention was drawn to an object on a table in the corner. The room also had a wind-up gramophone. Gloria's stomach did a double flip!

'Yes,' admitted Mrs Lewis, noting her interest. 'We sure likes to offer our clients the most up-to-date facilities.'

But this gramophone wasn't a patch on Gloria's own. Not only was it much smaller, it didn't even have a horn. The music apparently came out of the lid. Oh well, not much chance of being slurped up by this one!

So they had supper with the Lewis family. A thick, creamy broth, home-made rolls, cheese and fresh fruit. It was delicious.

Mr Lewis kept conversation rolling during the meal. It turned out he was a train driver, an express-train driver, which meant he was often away from home. But he loved his job.

'And I've just been promoted, yes sir,' he told the girls proudly. 'The night service from Cincinnati to New York, no less!'

'Really?' Gloria answered, taking care to roll her 'r' and stick to one word.

'Three times a week at ten-fifteen. Of course we have to clock on half an hour beforehand to check the motor's firing properly – and then we're away.'

'Bed!' Gloria announced, getting decisively to her feet and guessing Susie would follow. And instead of saying, 'Good night,' which would have been two words, she merely nodded to them, then smiled and left the room. You can get a lot of mileage out of one word.

Even though she was thoroughly wrecked, Gloria couldn't sleep for quite a while. She started thinking again about her mum – it was funny the way she missed her more at night.

With all her heart, she hoped she was right in thinking that time was completely immobile in Sheffield. Her mum might be worried sick, might have got the police looking for her and Susie – it made her feel awful just to think about it.

Instead, she preferred to imagine her mum permanently crouching beside a filing cabinet at the town hall, Mrs Fisher parked on the settee, her jaws all set to crunch some nutty bread, and the frilly, roller-skating majorettes frozen in mid-sprint down the supermarket aisles.

If Gloria had been a bit better at maths, she might have been able to come up with a formula to *prove* that time couldn't possibly be moving in 1995. As it was, she tossed and turned. And then there was Willy to think about. Gloria wasn't a doctor. In fact, come to think of it, that was one of the rare professions she'd never considered becoming. Even she could see there was something wrong. Even she could see that Willy was getting weaker and weaker, that his cough was growing worse.

Susie was softly snoring. Sleep seemed to be steering well clear of Gloria that night. She tossed and turned in her bed. Worried about her mum and Willy. And like a needle in a record groove, she was stuck.

14   *Revenge!*
(in the form of a pillow fight)

Gloria and Susie were up bright and early the next morning and a bouquet of sunshine greeted them as they scurried down the Lewises' path. They were in for a shock when they arrived at Willy's place.

If there was one thing the girls had learned they could rely on Willy to do, it was to be first up in the morning. Sometimes it would drive Gloria mad. He'd come knocking on their door and it would be barely seven o'clock. Practically the middle of the night as far as Gloria was concerned.

But the landlady, who was busy crocheting in the sitting-room, informed them she hadn't heard Willy moving.

Susie gripped Gloria's hand. 'You don't think anything's happened to him, do you?' She was voicing Gloria's own fears.

Gloria couldn't even answer Susie, she just

shook her head furiously and dashed towards the stairs. Room number four, the landlady had said. Gloria tapped gently on the door. A heavy, gaping silence. They waited a few seconds more and stepped inside.

The curtains were drawn and the room was in darkness. The girls knocked into a table and a chair on their way over to Willy's bedside. Gradually, their eyes grew accustomed to the light. Willy was lying without a pillow, his head lolling to one side. He was absolutely still. His arms were spread across the covers. But it looked unnatural somehow. As though someone had been in and set him out in this position. He looked too much like a statue to be sleeping.

'Susie, I'm scared,' Gloria whispered.

'Touch his head. Make sure he's still . . . all right . . .' Susie always ducked out of taking risks.

Gloria swallowed but the lump in her throat sprang right back. Then, as she'd seen people do in loads of films, she bent to kiss his forehead.

'Fooled you that time!' Willy sang out, slyly opening an eye.

'Aaargh!' Gloria screamed, jumping out of her skin.

'Willy, you rotten thing! Scaring us to death like that,' Susie scolded, sitting down on the bed. Her heart was pounding so loud, she was dizzy.

'A guy decides to have a lie-in for once,' Willy chuckled, 'and his two best friends act like he's a corpse!' He was laughing so much it was making him splutter.

'Catch,' said Gloria, chucking a pillow in Susie's direction. 'One, two, three, wallop!'

By the end of the pillow-fight, not only had Willy promised never to pull the same stunt again, he was eating out of their hands.

15 *Drama in the tent*

Tent shows are amazing, Gloria was thinking to herself. I don't know why they ever got rid of them.

It was the interval and the atmosphere was still electric. The crowd had been whooping and cheering and joining in some of the numbers in the first half. That had never happened before. It had a lot to do with the tent layout. Benches were arranged in a horseshoe formation up to the edges of the flaps, which somehow seemed to make things much cosier. Right at the back stood a small platform, where the band were installed. But the bulk of the performance took place in 'the ring'. The rest of the performers were on ground level.

'Another five minutes, Miss Gloria,' Teagarden said, offering her some of his fruit soda. 'Say, there's a very famous gallery in Cincinnati you might like to visit . . .'

Gloria smiled. 'Perhaps,' she replied, knowing

full well she had no intention of going. Then she pointed with a grimace to her outfit which was the wrong one for their next routine and scuttled off.

She ran into Willy who was in the middle of another coughing bout. 'I'll be lucky . . . to get to the end of . . . this performance,' he panted.

Gloria gave him a helpful thump on the back. 'So long as you don't get any silly ideas of dropping dead in the middle of it. Otherwise we might just have to resort to the pillow treatment to resuscitate you.' She grinned and ran off to the Sunbeams' 'dressing-room', a small tent out the back.

Susie was putting the finishing touches to her eyes. 'Thought you couldn't face putting on your tail,' she said to Gloria, grinning.

'I'd better get a move on. We're on in three minutes!' And with that Gloria started shuffling into her cumbersome get-up.

Ever since Washington, the Sunbeams had opened the second half of the show with a new number, 'Every Little Fish in the Sea'. Dressed as, you guessed it, mermaids. The song always made Gloria think of her bedroom and Pucker swimming endlessly round or busy trying to hypnotise her.

The crowd adored them. Nobody seemed to mind that for once the mermaids were black. Nor that one or two of them, Gloria included, pulled faces as they pulled the combs through their hair. (Have you ever tried fine-combing frizzy hair?)

The lights went down to allow them all to flop, crawl and wriggle their way out of the ring.

Then it was time for Rosetta and Willy's tear-jerker. Rosetta was looking stunning as usual in her tight, backless, red dress as she wafted towards the microphone. Gloria, who was in the middle of pulling off her tail, sat at the sides and had a perfect view of the pair.

'Ladies and gentlemen,' Rosetta was saying in her husky sweet voice, 'I'd like to introduce my son, Willy Ray.'

The audience cheered and stamped. The band struck up the intro to 'Rainbow Promised Land'. Gloria was watching every move. And, as if in slow-motion, she witnessed Willy stagger slightly, then fall forwards on the ground! For one second, she thought it was another trick, another game, Willy the tease. But even Willy wouldn't take things this far and pretend to collapse in front of thousands of people.

Rosetta crouched over her son and wailed. The crowd was in an uproar. Teagarden seemed to leap from the bandstand and scoop Willy up in his arms.

'Get a taxi to my place,' Gloria said. 'Lewises' Hotel, Cade Long Alley. There's a doctor right next door.'

16 *Get-well wishes sent*

'Where am I?' Willy moaned again and again, rousing enough to be asking questions.

'Sugar, you're safe. Don't worry about anything.' Rosetta squeezed his hand and sniffed back her tears.

Dr Mitchell checked Willy's eyes, his pulse, his temperature. Then she listened to Willy's chest and heart and gently tried to get him to bend his legs. 'Willy, can you tell me what happened?'

'I was on-stage, I hadn't even begun the number with Mom.' Willy's voice was rough and hoarse. 'Then the lights started coming towards me – and my head, I couldn't move my head. Then I woke up here.'

'Thanks, Willy. That's all I need to know.' The doctor walked into the corridor and Rosetta followed.

Gloria could hear them talking in muffled voices and picked out the words 'severe exhaustion', 'lung infection', 'possible tuberculosis' and 'danger list' as clear as the day. Her heart nearly did a somersault. Danger list, what did that mean? Willy was going to be all right, wasn't he? They must be able to make him get better. Antibiotics, had they been discovered in 1929? Willy had to pull through, he had to get better fast.

He was lying there, rasping a little. Gloria could see pearls of sweat on his forehead and neck. She tiptoed closer. She had no intentions of trying to kiss him again! 'Willy, can you hear me?' Her voice was no more than a whisper. Was he asleep or just too ill to take in her words? Gloria tried again. 'Look, you've got to get better fast. I'll give anything, anything, I'll even stay here if you want me to but, please, Willy, just get well.'

17 *Gloria's conscience rent*

Gloria sat beside Willy, lost in thought. She didn't notice Rosetta and Dr Mitchell go quietly down into the kitchen. But, upset though she was, she couldn't mistake the thundering footsteps of Susie charging upstairs. The bedroom door flew open.

'Gloria, is he all right?' she panted.

'No thanks to us,' Gloria answered, not looking at her. 'If we hadn't beaten him up with the pillows this morning . . .'

'It was a joke, Gloria. How were we to know Willy was so run-down? After pulling that stunt on us,' Susie said.

'It's a lung infection, TB possibly, that's what the doctor said, Susie,' and Gloria's voice had a funny little quiver in it, 'do they know how to cure TB in 1929?'

Susie looked at Willy lying lifeless on the bed. 'Bound to,' she bluffed. 'Ooh, forgot to tell you, Reed's going mad! Rosetta gone, Willy gone, you gone. He says he wants you to do two of Willy's songs for tonight's performance.'

'Why me?' Gloria demanded.

Susie blushed. 'Thought I'd put in a good word. This could be your big break, Gloria,' she said, slightly apologetically.

Gloria snorted. 'I'm not budging from Willy's bedside! Willy could be dying for all Reed knows and all he can think about is tonight's performance! Why don't you do it?'

Susie continued in a quiet voice, 'Gloria, I can't sing. You're always telling me what a disaster area my voice is!'

Gloria couldn't suppress a giggle. 'Like a parrot having its neck wrung,' she mumbled.

'Worse,' admitted Susie. 'Anyway, Reed wants the pair of us to do one of those "wile an' wonnerful" dance sequences' (Susie's American accent was quite good by now) 'we did for the audition as well.'

'"Jungle Jamboree"?' asked Gloria, whose eyes had begun shining at the very mention. Fortunately, before she could get very far with her difficult decision – should she stick with her pal or head for an hour's fame? – Rosetta, Dr Mitchell, a nurse and two ambulance attendants all trooped into the room.

'They're moving my boy Willy to the hospital,' Rosetta explained, as the two angular men lifted Willy like a bale of hay off the bed and on to a stretcher. His breathing seemed to have eased a little. He was in a deep sleep.

'Best thing for him,' explained Dr Mitchell. 'The most up-to-date treatment.'

Oh, yeah, thought Gloria and winked at Susie.

'It's a fever hospital,' the doctor explained. 'For safety reasons, no one under the age of sixteen is allowed to visit.' It was like being hit on the chin with a brick. Gloria was knocked out.

'And round-the-clock care,' added Rosetta in too much of a fluster to notice. 'My lipstick, my lipstick, have either of you two seen my lipstick?'

Gloria frowned (fancy thinking of lipstick at a time like this!) and Susie shrugged and Rosetta bobbed downstairs after the others.

Things happen so fast sometimes. This morning Willy had seemed sick, then it turned out he was just messing about, playing the clown as usual. And now his life really was dangling by a thread!

'We can't do anything for him now,' Susie

said, guessing Gloria's thoughts. 'We've just got to keep our fingers crossed. We may as well go to the tent and do tonight's second show.'

Gloria threw her an angry look.

'"Jungle Jamboree" will take our minds off things,' Susie coaxed. 'After all, the show must go on.'

18   *Gloria, the star*

Gloria ended up deputising for Willy for six performances. Her singing was smashing, 'Jungle Jamboree' always brought the house down and even appearing with Rosetta (Gloria had to replace Willy for 'Rainbow Promised Land') was pleasant enough. 'I'd like to introduce a close friend of my boy Willy. Ladies and gentlemen, let's hear it for Gloria Esprit!' Those were Rosetta's very words night after night. And it's true, performing was fun. It was nice hearing people shout 'Bravo!' and 'Encore!' and 'More!'

Six performances. In the end, you take everything in your stride, Gloria realised. She also realised with a jolt that fame meant *nothing, nothing at all* when a friend was at death's door in hospital.

Sunday was a day of rest. And even though Gloria and Susie doubted very much that they'd be allowed in, they decided to head over to the fever hospital anyway.

The gate-keeper, a wizened little man with a white moustache and a thin layer of white curls, was adamant. 'Orders is orders. It'd be more than my job's worth, letting in two gals,' he informed them flatly.

'And free tickets to Reed's Rollicking Rhythm Show and our autographs couldn't tempt you . . .' This was Gloria's last (and only) card.

'We're part of the Sunbeams. And Gloria here's a solo star.'

He seemed to be softening. 'OK, sign here, Sunbeams. I can always say you sneaked in while I was picking up garbage.'

They were in!

Willy was on the third floor, Rosetta had already told them that. Up the stairs they ran. Into a large airy room with forty beds or more that were all hidden away behind curtains.

'Where do we start?' Gloria asked Susie. 'It'll take half an hour to find him in here.'

'You take one side. I'll take the other,' Susie told her.

And in fact it only took five minutes to find Willy's bed.

'Look who's here,' Rosetta exclaimed, when Gloria poked her head round the curtains.

'Hey,' she went on, 'thought you two were too young to visit.'

Gloria decided not to get into a complicated discussion with Rosetta, beckoned to Susie, then sat down at Willy's bedside. 'Willy, how you feeling?' she asked, gently.

Willy turned his head slowly towards her. 'Alive,' he retorted and reached for her hand.

'Willy's doing fine,' Rosetta nipped in. 'The doctors can't believe how quickly he's recovering.'

'You're looking better than that day you collapsed,' Susie told him, wanting to sound encouraging.

'Tell them, Mom. Go on. I want them to be first to know.'

Rosetta poked her head outside the curtains to check that no one was within earshot. Then, in a quiet voice, she informed them, 'Willy and I have reached a momentous decision. We're leaving the show. The doctors say Willy's fit to travel first class. We're heading on home. Tomorrow night.'

Gloria blinked. 'Home?' she repeated blankly. 'You can't just walk out on the show!'

'There'll be other shows, other cities,' Rosetta replied dramatically. 'My boy needs me now.

Not in three months' time. So it's first stop Harlem, second stop Tuscaloosa.'

'Willy, what about us?' Susie asked. But deep down Gloria already knew the answer to that one. Their number was up. They'd been in the right place at the right time. Bridged a gap when the show needed them. If Willy and Rosetta were jumping ship, then they would too. And try their very best to make it back to their home.

19 Goodbye, so long, so far

'Listen here, gal,' Mrs Lewis said, the very next night. 'I don't know where you come from with that fancy accent of yours –' Gloria flushed to the roots of her hair '– but here in Cincinnati, the word hospitality means something. And so does helping folks in distress. It's been an honour for us to have Rosetta Ray under our roof. So just put your money back in your purse.'

They'd actually travelled from Cincinnati on the 10.15 night service using complimentary first-class tickets, courtesy of Mr Lewis. In fact, the Lewises had been wildly generous with them. They'd provided them all with free board and lodging for over a week until Willy was well enough to leave hospital. When Gloria tried to persuade Mrs Lewis to accept something, she'd wagged a finger at her.

No point in arguing. Things fell into place like jigsaw pieces in a puzzle. Even if some of them hurt more than others . . . Like saying goodbye to Willy. Two days they spent, trotting through the streets of Harlem behind Rosetta who wanted to stock up on bits and pieces that she wouldn't be able to find down south, such as various shades of lipsticks!

Traipsing about at least meant that Gloria and Susie discovered four gramophone stores and promised they would call back soon. But two days rushing about on Rosetta's heels and packing chests and crates meant hardly any time with Willy, who was resting in bed.

The night before Willy and his mom were due to leave Gloria managed to get a moment alone with him. Rosetta had rushed off with Susie to have her hair and her nails done.

Anyway, it gave Gloria a chance to have a few uninterrupted words with the invalid.

'Willy, I feel terrible,' Gloria announced, holding out a frothy cup of hot chocolate. It was eight o'clock.

'Hey, I'm supposed to be the one with tuberculosis,' joked Willy. 'How come you're feeling terrible?'

'You know what I mean. I'm upset. You're leaving in the morning. I'll probably never see you again!'

'Gloria, don't do this to me,' Willy grinned.

106

'Don't start turning all sentimental and acting like a girl!'

'Aaagh!' yelled Gloria and they both collapsed into laughter.

'You two'll be heading off soon yourselves.' Willy placed his cup on the bedside table. 'Just as soon as you locate another one of those magic gramophones.'

'There's bound to be one on every street corner. Knowing us, we'll be stuck here for another fifty years . . . until we're born.'

Willy laughed. 'You'll sort something, Gloria. I know you will.'

'I'm glad you're so optimistic,' she answered glumly.

'We're friends, Gloria. We've always looked out for each other. Why, you even stood in for me in the show!'

'Friends,' repeated Gloria. 'What good are friends who live thousands of miles and several decades apart?'

'This'll stand the test of time. Believe me.'

Gloria wanted to very much indeed.

The test of time, the test of time. Gloria kept saying it over and over again in her head in the taxi at the crack of dawn next morning. Even though it was a luxury, they'd never have made it on the streetcar with all that luggage. But the taxi made the journey shorter, brought their separation nearer.

Rosetta said, 'You gals sure you can't come with us?'

Gloria shook her head. 'We have to set off home ourselves,' she answered loosely.

Willy threw her a quick, sad look.

Leaving people you care about is hard at the best of times. But even the test of time won't let you travel through space and across sixty years any day of the week. Gloria couldn't imagine how she'd ever see any of them again. She wouldn't even be able to send them a Christmas card! What can you say to people you're leaving for good?

The majestic Grand Central Station came into view. Gloria's heart sank deeper. She didn't feel like admiring architecture today.

'Stay in the apartment as long as you wish,' Rosetta said. She was perky, cheerful, glad, after all, to be returning to her home-town. 'Rent's paid up till the end of December.'

'Thanks,' muttered Susie. December!

'And I wanted to give you this,' Rosetta went on. She reached into the bag beside her legs and handed them a record. It was a signed copy of 'August Sunset'.

'We've got it already,' Susie said before Gloria nudged her one.

'There must be some mistake,' Rosetta informed her. 'The record's not being released until next month.'

Susie didn't argue. Anyway, the record they had in Sheffield hadn't been personally signed.

Once out of the taxi, they were carried along in the station's hectic movement. They called a porter, queued for tickets, then set off for the train.

'Gloria,' Willy whispered, 'isn't there any address you could let me have?'

'Where I live wasn't built for another fifty years!' Gloria told him miserably. 'And post offices only keep letters a few months, not a lifetime.' But there had to be a solution, there had to be some way of keeping in touch.

'Great-aunt Lariss!' Gloria exclaimed as they neared platform seven. Maybe it wouldn't work, but it was worth a try. Aunt Lariss, Gloria knew, had lived in the same house all her life and, according to Gloria's mum, she was over seventy. 'She's my aunt, my great-aunt in Jamaica, the one who sent me the gramophone in the first place,' she added, with a wink.

Once they got to the train – a dark green one this time, Gloria borrowed a pen and paper from the porter and jotted the address she'd seen written over and over on the crate: Gloria Esprit (she put first of all), c/o Larissa Esprit, The Wood House, Moon Creek, Jamaica.

She handed it to Willy, who nodded. A long, slow, painful nod. Then there were kisses and hugs all round and Rosetta was sniffing and pulling out her powder puff and dabbing her nose and sniffing some more. And Susie amazed them all by bellowing. Through her own misty eyes, Gloria watched them climb on the train and heard Rosetta saying, 'Such charming girls, Willy. Make sure you keep in touch.'

The doors slammed, clatter, clatter, clatter. The whistle blew. The train pulled out. And Gloria ached all over. It's always easier leaving than being left.

20 *Banana milk-shake, chocolate corn pie*

'Sooz, this place never used to echo,' Gloria remarked, sprawling on the settee. It was eleven o'clock. Willy and Rosetta had been gone three hours.

'I know. It's giving me the spooks,' Susie answered, sighing. 'I bet I've missed the birth and everything. Mum said I could see the baby as soon as it popped out.'

'Well, there's nothing to hang around here for any more. Let's go home, Susie.'

'You make it sound simple. Like all we have to do is press a button!'

'Don't let the present carry you away too far, too fast, just make it last,' chanted Gloria and got up to look out of the window. Out in 125th Street, the group of girls were giggling and playing 'The Sea is Calm'.

'Oh, not Great-aunt Lariss's rhyme again,' Susie said. 'I mean, this has gone on long enough, don't you think?'

'Exactly,' exclaimed Gloria. 'Come on, let's check out some of those record shops.' And grabbing Rosetta's record on the way out, they set off.

'What time is it?' Susie asked for the third time in half an hour, after they'd been strolling through the leafy streets for what seemed like hours.

'Ten to one,' Gloria answered flatly. Three gramophone shops, no luck.

'It's playing tricks. It's slowed right down!' Susie declared.

'Maybe time would move faster if we did,' Gloria suggested. 'Come on, there's only one more shop on my list.'

It was tucked away in a tiny back street in Harlem. And it was wonderful! There were shiny saxophones and rows of banjos, small drums, medium drums, big drums, tambourines, triangles, trombones.

'And gramophones?' Gloria enquired politely. The other day it had certainly looked promising. 'Do you have any gramophones?'

'Sorry, ma'am,' the wrinkled shopkeeper replied. 'Try Marshall's, on 116th. They have the best selection in town.'

And it was true. Marshall's must have had

fifty different types of gramophone and hundreds and hundreds of radio sets.

Susie and Gloria had long since agreed they needed to find the self-same model.

'We're looking for a gramophone with a giant golden horn.' Susie spoke to the tall assistant whose neck was so long she reminded Gloria of a giraffe.

'Know the make?' the woman wanted to know.

'Her Mistress's Voice – there's a picture of a cat on the label . . . It might have been made in Jamaica.' Gloria racked her brains for information.

The woman shook her head firmly. 'Know the one you mean. It's a 1922 model, very rare indeed. Sorry, can't help you.' And she couldn't even suggest any other shops.

Gloria and Susie were gutted. Were they to be stranded in Harlem for ever? On a wild-goose chase for a gramophone that nobody sold any more?

Despondently, they trudged along 116th, not saying a word. The cherry reds, blues, peppermints and peaches of the shop blinds along here – the baker's, butcher's, candy store, shoe shops – clashed with their mood. There was even a billowing rainbow-coloured blind which, from a distance, looked like a beautiful giant butterfly. It turned out to be a bookshop with an impressive display of cookery books in the window.

'Mind if we call in there?' Gloria asked.

And in they trooped. There must have been hundreds of books on food. Not like the ones you get nowadays with bright, glossy, tongue-tempting photos. These were all text but the recipes had exciting names and loads of handy hints.

Gloria's attention was drawn to one called *The Infinite Cake Book*. It listed forty basic cake-making techniques but pointed out that there was no limit to the number of additional ingredients each recipe might include. Hence the audacious title. Mrs Fisher and her one-cake repertoire sprang to mind. Gloria yielded to temptation . . .

. . . And did something very, very impulsive indeed. In fact, in view of their limited finances (Reed had refused to pay them all their wages, claiming they'd broken their contract), talk about reckless! She marched over to the cash desk and, without even consulting Susie, who was browsing in the animals' section, she bought the very expensive book.

Back in the street, Susie was furious. 'Chuck all our money away, why don't you!' she yelled at Gloria. Sometimes when Susie raged, Gloria had the distinct impression she was just messing about. 'And why don't we have coffee and cakes while we're at it?' Susie went on.

Gloria thought she'd better humour her and trotted after her into the coffee shop which was right next door. The Blue Mountain Coffee Shop, it was called, and the proprietor was a black woman with a wonky grin.

'Make mine a banana milk-shake and two pieces of chocolate corn pie,' Susie said, provocatively.

'Sure, honey.' The woman set to work straight away. 'Anything for your friend?'

Gloria shook her head furiously. 'Susie, look, I'm sorry. Don't know what came over me,' she mumbled. 'But going mad in here's not going to make things any . . .' She didn't finish her sentence. She couldn't. Because, out of the corner of her eye, at the far end of the counter, she saw something that took all her breath away.

It was a magnificent mahogany gramophone with a gigantic horn. And it was the spitting image of Gloria's.

'Do you see what I see?' Gloria's voice had turned to a whisper. 'Tell me I'm not dreaming!'

'You're not. It's there all right,' Susie reassured her.

'You gals want music, jas' say the word.'

'We've, er, got our own record. Can we listen to that?'

The woman nodded and got on with cutting the cake.

'I suppose we'd better pay her now, while we still can,' Susie said in a low voice, realising the full implications of what was going on.

'That'll be one dollar fifteen, honey.' The woman had a sing-song voice. 'But there's no hurry. We ain't about to be blown down in a hurricane!' And she laughed. A broad, sunny laugh which reminded Gloria of her mum on a good day. Come to think of it, her face was *incredibly* similar to her mum's. Susie laid the money on the counter anyway.

'Yes, honey,' the woman continued, as though she could read Gloria's mind, 'me sure is from Jamaica. Belle Esprit's my name ...' Gloria's heart thudded. This woman must be her relative, her ancestor. 'Came over to Harlem three years ago. Left my three lickle gals back home ...' It looked as if Gloria and Susie were in for the woman's life story.

'You wouldn't have a daughter Larissa by any chance, would you?' Gloria couldn't resist fitting another piece into the puzzle.

'You gals ain't from Jamaica, so how come you know my baby?'

'Baby?' Gloria questioned.

'Be five in January. I ain't seen her since she was two.'

'Want a piece of cake, it's brill?' Susie asked Gloria. 'Or is it time to make a move?'

'I couldn't,' Gloria told her. Her stomach was churning like a storm at sea. Too many things to take in.

So they stood, picked up their book-shop carriers and shuffled down to the edge of the counter. Susie wound up the gramophone. Gloria slipped the record from its sleeve and placed it on the velvety brown turntable.

'What if it doesn't work?' Susie was suddenly frightened, and panicked.

'It will. It has to,' Gloria said steadily. Then she flicked the switch that made the turntable spin, and carefully lowered the arm. There was a dry hiss that grew and grew into a wind that twisted through the shop.

'Lordy, feels like a hurricane comin',' Belle

cried and rushed over to shut the door to keep this strange wild energy at bay.

Then the sax crooned, the piano rippled and Rosetta's sweet, haunting voice enveloped them once more. 'Au-Au-Au-August sunset from the moment we met . . .' Spin, spin, spin, went the turntable, and the whirlwind-hurricane buzzed and whipped round faster and faster and faster.

Spin, spin, spin. And *zoop*! One after another – Gloria first this time, Susie second – they split.

21   *Back home with a sigh*

Plop, plop plop went the plump raindrops on the windowpane. This was Sheffield, Gloria's bedroom! It was raining! They were home!

They'd shot along the same corridors of mauve and pale blue light. And this time the journey had seemed twice as long. But when you're homeward bound, things always drag. Another trick of time.

'Gloria, we did it! We're home!' Susie squealed in sheer delight. She had chocolate all over her face. And they were both dressed in American twenties style.

'Let's tidy ourselves up as fast as we can,' Gloria told her. 'We need to find out how long we've been missing. The police could be after us.'

Gloria rushed over to Pucker. She was terrified in case he'd been a victim of neglect, in case her mum had forgotten to feed him and he'd gone up to the great tank in the sky. But there he was, pelting about as large as life, and looking all set to have a whirl at hypnotising Gloria, if she'd give him half a chance. Phew!

'Got any leggings you can lend me?' Susie asked. 'Preferably purple ones?'

With her habitual difficulty, Gloria dug (being the operative word) out some gear. Her drawers were not the neatest you could imagine! And her mum hadn't rifled them in her absence, which was a good sign.

Wearing contemporary clothes again looked and felt most peculiar. Dresses can grow on you, Gloria realised with horror! When Susie nipped into the bathroom to clean up her face, Gloria tiptoed into her mum's bedroom to check the time. The digital clock said 16.49 which also looked promising. But there was no date.

'Glo,' Susie had got into the habit of using Willy's shortened form of Gloria too, 'what's that funny smell?'

'Nutty bread, Mrs Fisher's fresh-baked nutty bread,' Gloria told her. Some things hadn't changed. And if Mrs Fisher was up to the usual and the television was blaring out, didn't that mean, didn't that mean . . .? 'Give me a sec.' She suddenly remembered something she needed and popped back into her bedroom.

120

In the living-room Mrs Fisher was perched on the settee, a plate upon her lap. 'Ready for tea, you two? I've got some nutty bread jus' coolin',' she casually remarked, without taking her eyes off the set. Definitely not the welcome from someone who'd been separated from them for the last seven weeks!

'Want a piece, Sooz?' Gloria asked, hoping Susie would follow her into the kitchen so they could talk.

'Not after all that choccy cake I've just pigged myself with,' Susie said, winking. 'We dancers have got to watch our figures!'

Lost in a tangle of thoughts on her way into the kitchen, Gloria nearly walked straight into the crate that had delivered the gramophone. It was just where they'd left it! Which meant, thought Gloria, chomping on a slice of bread, no time had passed at all.

'I'd better get off home, Glo.' Susie got to her feet.

Gloria followed her to the door. 'They haven't noticed we've been gone weeks!' she exclaimed.

'I know. Weird, isn't it?' Susie said quietly. 'And you know what, it'll take me a few days to adapt to being back.'

They just looked at each other for a few seconds. Then Susie pushed a book into Gloria's hands. There was no photo on the cover, just the title which was *Your Pet Can Talk!*.

'It was in the bargain basket at the bookshop,' Susie explained. 'Nothing too extravagant!'

'You mean you were just pretending to be angry at the coffee shop?' Hardly anyone dared pull the wool over Big G's eyes!

'Oh, Gloria, couldn't you tell it was a wind-up?' Susie was all giggles.

Even though they hardly ever kissed or hugged, and even though Gloria was generally the queen when it came to teasing, she flung her arms round Susie and squeezed her tight. 'I've got a lot to thank you for, Sooz,' she told her.

Susie looked puzzled.

'Not just the book for Pucker. If you hadn't known about jazz and wanted to hear Rosetta's record, none of this would ever have happened.' She laughed. 'In fact, I would have gone on believing people in the past had dead-boring lives!'

'How many records did your auntie send you?' Susie was all smiles. 'How many adventures to go?'

Right that second, it didn't bear thinking about.

22   Mrs Fisher's reply

'Mrs Fisher,' Gloria yelled at the top of her voice when the adverts were on, 'Happy birthday!'

Mrs Fisher unwrapped the kitchen foil which was all Gloria had been able to lay her hands on at such short notice. And gasped in delight.

'*The Infinite Cake Book*!' she exclaimed. 'Chile, thank you!' And she planted a wet kiss on Gloria's cheek, then started flicking eagerly through the pages. 'All these new nutty bread recipes,' she told Gloria, who hadn't quite anticipated such a response, 'them goin' keep me up to me elbows in palm oil for years to come!'

The rain rattled the windowpanes. It sounded like a storm was brewing. Years and years more nutty bread, thought Gloria with a grimace. At least, thanks to *Your Pet Can Talk!*, she'd be able to air her feelings about it with Pucker and hear his views. Anyway, sometimes you've got to take what life hands you on a plate.

The End (almost!)

Happylogue

Tuscaloosa, 10 April 1930, was the postmark on the yellowing envelope that had been sent all the way to Jamaica.

Gloria had come across it quite by chance when, all a-tingle, she was placing 'August Sunset' back in the case with all the other records (which she didn't even dare look at for the time being). It had somehow slipped inside.

'*Hi, gals,*' he'd written (that afternoon, Gloria could forgive Willy joking about with the 'gals' business).

Hope this letter finds you home and well. I'm just about fully recovered and making the most of this quiet spell. Not that it looks like being quiet for too long. Just as soon as she thinks I'm rested and fit enough, Mom's planning to check out New Orleans. There are loadsa clubs and theaters so no shortage of work. But having time with Mom and not just talking about the next routine, the next song (why, we even go walking out together as the sun sets – the April sunset!), I can't say how precious it all is to me. Fingers crossed we get to stay calm and cosy together till the end of summer. (I was always an optimist!)

There's loads to see and do. And I've made friends here. But I want you to know, Susie and Gloria, that you're always in my thoughts. Sometimes I run out at night, look at the moon and think of you both, years and years away. Then I wish I could travel through time. Don't you worry about not writing back – it's enough that I know this letter from me will bring you much joy. And that you care as much as you do.

And if you're ever feeling blue, just yell out, 'Test of time'. You can rest assured I'll have done it hundreds of times too.

Kisses from Rosetta who figures you're in Jamaica. There's some stuff mothers just can't understand.

All my affection,
Your friend,
Willy Ray

Gloria couldn't think what to do. Run over to Susie's place? Didn't feel like her legs had the energy to carry her there. Lie down on her bed and try not to scream, 'It's not fair, it's not fair, it's not fair!' Or even, 'Test of time, test of time, test of time!'?

At moments like this, she was very grateful for Pucker's company. Learning to talk was not proving to be one of his fortes but Gloria reckoned he was still quite capable of putting her in a trance. Then she'd be able to move again through time (which, as Gloria was beginning to see more and more, is entirely in the mind). Or at least stop feeling pain.

Pucker was in a cheerful mood and wriggled and squirmed in his bowl. Willy wouldn't want me to mope, thought Gloria. Maybe some of Pucker's *joie de vivre* was rubbing off on her. So for the next half an hour or so, though no one was counting, Gloria danced about in her room, wriggling and squirming, pretending she was a goldfish in a bowl. Little by little, it banished her gloom. Then she fell to the floor, laughing. Because as she was dancing, even if Gloria didn't have all the answers right then and there, she suddenly saw that true friends stick with you. (Test of time and all that.) For ever.

The End (no kidding!)